# PROMISES IN EVERY STAR

## AN EROTIC COLLECTION

**Edited by Todd Gregory for Bold Strokes Books**

Rough Trade

Blood Sacraments

Wings: Subversive Gay Angel Erotica

Sweat: Gay Jock Erotica

Raising Hell: Demonic Gay Erotica

**Visit us at www.boldstrokesbooks.com**

# PROMISES IN EVERY STAR

## AN EROTIC COLLECTION

*by*

Todd Gregory

A Division of Bold Strokes Books

2013

**PROMISES IN EVERY STAR: AN EROTIC COLLECTION**
© 2013 By Todd Gregory. All Rights Reserved.


ISBN 13: 978-1-60282-787-5


This Trade Paperback Original Is Published By
Bold Strokes Books, Inc.
P.O. Box 249
Valley Falls, NY 12185

First Edition: February 2013

---

**Credits**
Editor: Stacia Seaman
Production Design: Stacia Seaman
Cover Design by Sheri (graphicartist2020@hotmail.com)

This is for Matt Valletta, Brandon Benson,
and the ReVision boys

# CONTENTS

# INTRODUCTION

I'd never once considered using a pseudonym.

Part of this was my own boundless egotism; what was the point of publishing if my real name wasn't on the work? I know there are authors who use pseudonyms—and that is their choice and their right; whatever their reasoning, I consider it to be valid. But for me, I wanted to see my real name listed as the author of the short story in the anthology or the magazine where it appeared, or on the spine of the novel so I could look at it on the bookshelf and smile to myself with pride: *See there? On that bookshelf? That's my NAME on that book, because I wrote it.*

Back in the days before I started publishing, I couldn't even conceive of using a name other than my own.

My very first sale of fiction—any fiction—was an erotic wrestling story to an anthology called *Men for All Seasons* (an anthology that is sadly long out of print), and around the same time, I sold another erotic wrestling story to *Men* magazine. Despite being told by any number of established writers that I was making an enormous mistake, I refused to use a pseudonym for either story—they were my first fiction sales, and I'd been waiting all of my life to make them. There was simply no way in heaven or hell those stories were going into print without MY name on them. Only a few months later

I sold my first novel, *Murder in the Rue Dauphine*, and my career was off and running. I also sold a proposal to edit an erotic anthology, *Full Body Contact,* around the same time. Again, I did this book under my own name, and signed to do another erotica anthology, *FRATSEX.*

Between those two stories first seeing print in August 2000 and the release of *FRATSEX* in June 2004, I published several more erotic wrestling stories as well as three other novels. I was building a career—even reaching the enviable position of having editors ask me to write stories for their anthologies—when I began to notice something.

The requests were, without fail, for me to write a wrestling story.

I also had started pitching ideas for novels that weren't mysteries to my publishers, only to have the proposals rejected…and invariably, the rejection would ask about the proposal for another mystery.

I'd been told by many writers that publishers and readers label authors; that once you're a "mystery writer" in the business, all anyone would ever want from you is another mystery, and that readers would even feel *betrayed* if I wrote something else. I had already begun to notice that my mysteries were being categorized as "erotic mysteries" (they weren't); I was even informed on a mystery panel at Saints and Sinners one year by the moderator that my novels were "full of sex" (they aren't).

I began to realize that I might have done myself a disservice by not using a pseudonym to write and edit erotica; but I also felt a little defiant. *I'll write what I damned well please, thank you very much, and if you have a problem with it—well, that's your problem, isn't it?*

And I wanted to write other things besides wrestling erotica, frankly.

I wanted to break out of the box I was being put in as *Greg Herren.*

I wanted to write other things.

So, I decided to write a story and use the name "Todd Gregory."

My full birth name is Gregory Todd Herren, so it's not hard to see how I came up with the name. (I'd already used another pseudonym to write some paranormal short stories, but that is a story for another time.) I wanted to write a story based loosely on an experience I had on a beach in Hawaii when I was single, and it had a bit of a paranormal edge to it. That story, "The Sea Where It's Shallow," was originally published on the Velvet Mafia web-magazine, and the response to it was really amazing. I had been writing short stories for years at this point, and not being able to get them published anywhere—the market for gay-themed short fiction that wasn't about sex was slim to the point of nonexistent.

It occurred to me I could, however, publish them if I added a sex scene to them and sold them as gay erotica.

And so that's how I came to start publishing and editing under the name Todd Gregory.

I've never hidden the fact that I am Todd Gregory, and it always surprises me when someone doesn't know that Todd Gregory is, in fact, Greg Herren. This actually worked so well that I considered resurrecting my paranormal pseudonym; I took on another pseudonym to continue writing wrestling erotica (which is yet another story for another time). Now each aspect of my writing career is successfully compartmentalized and branded with three different names. I have continued to edit anthologies of gay erotica under the Todd Gregory brand, and will continue to do so (I just signed a contract for another). The Todd Gregory name has also been useful as a novelist; I have at this time published two gay erotic romances under that name, and a third is in production at the time of this writing.

Some of the stories in this collection were originally published under the Greg Herren name, but when going through my files to cull a collection, I realized that those stories *would* have been Todd Gregory stories had I thought to use a pseudonym at the time. I wanted to include those stories here, and so have rebranded them. "Promises in Every Star" is one of those stories, and so is "The Porn King and I." "Unsent" was written as a Todd Gregory story, but when it was submitted the editor wanted me to use my own name for it, so I did. Despite that, I have always thought of it as a Todd Gregory story. Some of these stories were sold to anthologies that never saw print, or came and went rather quickly; I certainly hope you enjoy them.

I have also included a couple of stories that have never been published as some lagniappe for you, Constant Reader. Many times I will be asked to contribute a story to an anthology and will start writing it, only to set it aside to work on something else. Time management being a serious issue for me, this happens a lot more times than I care to admit. It always bothers me, though, to leave something unfinished. I'll often finish the story even though the deadline has passed—figuring another opportunity will present itself at some point. I am using this collection as one of those opportunities—and am using it to move some stories from the unfinished pile to the finished.

So, here you go, the Todd Gregory short story canon. These aren't all of them, and there will certainly be many more of them, I hope.

Enjoy!

Greg Herren
New Orleans, September 2012

## PROMISES IN EVERY STAR

There's nothing quite like the smell of a cornfield after a heavy rain.

I'd forgotten that smell in the twenty-five years or so since I'd left Kansas and never looked back. Off in the east, I could see black clouds and the mist hanging like a curtain from them to the ground, making everything on the other side blurry as though hidden behind gauze. I'd forgotten how the sky in Kansas surrounds you and seems to just go on forever, and how you could see the weather coming and the weather that had already been. There were no clouds overhead now, just sky a color somewhere between azure and robin's egg, reaching down into the wet corn. The pavement of the county road beneath the tires of my rented red Mustang convertible was wet, splashing every once in a while, with the water being thrown up making a slight slapping sound against the rubber.

Twenty-five years. What else had I forgotten?

As I turned off onto the Carterville road, I slid Fleetwood Mac's *Rumours* into the CD player and turned it up. This was the way I used to drive to school when Mom let me take the car or one of my friends picked me up so I didn't have to ride the bus. It was a CD now rather than a scratchy 8-track player, and the sound quality was much better, but it was still the same music. I smiled to myself as I pictured my old green 1969

Chevrolet Bel Air, with holes rusted in the sides driving up the Carterville Road, its old muffler pipe hanging too low to the ground in the back. All the windows would be open to catch the breeze and eliminate the smell of the cigarette dangling from my lip. Stevie would be wailing about the thunder, and the rain washing you clean, and you'll know. I would sing along at the top of my lungs, thumping my hand on the steering wheel in time with the bass line.

*No, it doesn't look too different*, I thought as the Mustang sped along. It seemed like it was the same fields, the same houses, and the same barns. Every once in a while there'd be a clearing in the corn and a brick house I didn't remember would appear, laundry flapping in the sweet after-rain air on a clothesline, a couple of cars in the unpaved drive. I crossed the bridge across the Cottonwood River and saw a house coming up on the right. *The Rosses used to live there*, I thought as I drove by. Mrs. Ross was the high school secretary, and Sue was her spoiled only child. I couldn't remember what Mr. Ross did for a living, but I remember Sue had her own custom Mustang when we were in school, and she always dressed nice. Sue was cute, in a little-girlish kind of way, and a lot of the guys thought she was sexy. I thought she was funny. She made me laugh. She also didn't strike me as the type who'd marry any of the boys in our school. Sue would, I thought even then, marry money.

The mailbox still said *ROSS*. I guessed the Rosses would probably be in their seventies by now, and why wouldn't they still be there? Sue was undoubtedly long gone, probably coming home a couple of times a year with her kids to see them, and every once in a while they'd get into their Buick and go see her.

I *was* curious to see my old classmates again after so many years. I wondered who would show up. I hadn't gone to either the ten- or the twenty-year, and still wasn't quite sure why I was coming to the twenty-fifth. But as I drew closer, each step of the long journey from New Orleans, I began experiencing some anticipation, a bit of excitement I hadn't dreamed I would feel, and every once in a while I found myself smiling.

I was definitely going to be the best- and youngest-looking man there. I felt relatively certain I was the only one who went to the gym at least three times a week. My head was shaved into a military-looking crew cut. Three years earlier I'd surrendered the battle to my receding hairline and gotten it shorn, and had never looked back from that decision.

It was the smartest thing I ever did. No more expensive stylists, blow-dryers, combs and brushes and gels and products and conditioners for me, thank you very much.

I looked down. I was wearing a white Calvin Klein tank T-shirt, tight in the chest and cut low on the shoulders. My jean shorts were about two sizes too big and rolled up at the knees. When I stood, they hung loosely off my hips. My contacts were in. I'd shaved that morning and trimmed my goatee. I was wearing brown suede work boots that reached just above my ankles. I smiled at myself in the rearview mirror. They would be completely oblivious to the fact I was dressed as a gay party boy clone.

It was also a safe bet I'd be the only one dressed this way.

Then again, I really had no idea what straight Kansans in their mid-forties were wearing these days. There was bound to be a Walmart in Kahola, the county seat. Did they drive SUVs? *That would be weird*, I thought, and laughed at myself. Just because I remembered Kansas as a foreign planet didn't mean it actually was one. Of course there were Walmarts in

Kansas; probably outlet malls as well. Car dealerships sold the same cars all over the country, so there would undoubtedly be some SUVs at the reunion.

Hell, there might even be a Lexus.

*Maybe*, I thought in a slight bit of a panic, *the rented Mustang convertible might be too much. Why didn't I just rent a compact car like I usually do whenever I travel?*

*Because you wanted to impress these people, these rustic back-country Kansas hicks who always made you feel like an outsider, that's why.*

The newsletter Jenna Bradley had sent out included everyone's current address, marital status, and how many kids they had. Of course, the letter Jenna had included only in mine also covered divorces, jail sentences, and alcohol problems. Out of a class of forty-eight, only six of us no longer lived in Kansas, and only twelve of us lived outside a hundred-mile radius of dear old Southern Heights High.

So, the outsider, the homo, the faggot, wanted to show up at the reunion in a totally bitchin' car, with about 6 percent body fat, and rub their noses in his sophistication and urban glamour.

*Oh, I'm a successful photographer just back from a fashion photo shoot in Milan. And what do you do?*

Of course, the shoot in Milan ran up all of my credit cards, and I was still waiting for my payment check.

But there was no need for them to know *that*, was there?

I crossed the railroad tracks and entered the teeming metropolis of Carterville, Kansas. The rusted metal sign right after the tracks read Carterville Population 84. After a couple of blocks, I came to the turn-off to Tony's house—well, where Tony *used* to live. I took a left, thinking *why the hell not* and there it was, the second house on the right, practically the same as it had been all those years ago.

Only now the mailbox said *MATHERS*, a name I didn't recognize. According to Jenna's newsletter, Tony now worked as a trash collector in Topeka.

Nice work if you can get it.

I hadn't asked Jenna if Tony was coming. She'd mentioned he had come to the ten and twenty, so it was fairly safe to assume he might come to the twenty-five. No one knew I was coming. Jenna was the only one I stayed in touch with via e-mail, and even that was very sporadic. Jenna and I had only reconnected prior to the twenty-year, and according to her gossipy report afterward, everyone was very curious about me.

I just bet they were.

I sat there, the car idling, looking at the dilapidated house. Surely that couldn't be the same battered screen door?

Christine McVie launched into "You Make Loving Fun."

I could see Tony just as clearly as if I'd seen him just yesterday. The first time I had seen him in his underwear, on a hot August afternoon right after football practice. He pulled on a pair of blue briefs with red trim. I'd never seen colored underwear before, and it hugged his white ass, outlining the cleft between the cheeks. His tanned muscular legs were covered with wiry black hair. Someone called his name from across the locker room and he turned with a big smile on his face, and the sight of his chest, thickly muscled with nipples the size of half dollars, made me catch my breath.

I fell in love in that moment; madly, passionately in love. For me, Tony was everything I could ever possibly want in a boy. I fantasized about kissing him on his thick sensual lips, tasting his tongue. I dreamed about him lying on top of me, my hands running down his broad back to where it narrowed, cupping his hard buttocks and squeezing. I wondered how his cock would taste in my mouth. There I was, the new kid, transferred in from Chicago, staring at this boy from across the locker room, not even caring if anyone was following my line of sight and noticed what I was staring at.

We had a couple of classes together, and there was, after all, football practice. I started making an attempt to befriend him, and it wasn't hard to do. For some reason, Tony wasn't particularly well liked either. I never wondered about it, was just grateful that he too was outside the "in-crowd," if such a small school could be said to have one—the arrogant jocks in our class who thought they were better than everyone else. They grudgingly tolerated me because I was a good football player, but made it very clear I wasn't part of their crowd. I wasn't invited to their parties or their get-togethers. Neither was Tony, so it was relatively easy for us to become friends. We also had a similar sense of humor. And whatever personality differences existed, my desire to be close to him heavily outweighed them. I hated his girlfriend, Allyson, because she took Tony's time and attention away from me. It was, of course, *her* fault Tony and I weren't together in the way that I wanted. We used to sleep over at each other's houses from time to time, to study together or work on papers.

I only stayed at Tony's house once or twice, though—he usually stayed at mine. I think he was a little ashamed of his family. His stepfather worked at the meat packing plant in the county seat; his mother worked as a housekeeper at the Best Western on the highway. Their house didn't have central heat or air; the wall that separated his bedroom from his parents' was just paneling nailed over studs with no soundproofing or insulation. His clothes were inexpensive and worn. My house, in the nearby town of Cottonwood Rapids, must have seemed palatial. Wall-to-wall carpeting, central heat and air, I had my own phone in my room, and my mother didn't have a job. He was always stunned by the meals my mother would come up with for dinner when he stayed over; beef burgundy, pepper steak and rice, chicken Kiev.

I used to sneak glances at him in the locker room and in the showers, taking photographs with my mental camera I could revisit later while masturbating. And sometimes, when he stayed over, we would wrestle in our underwear; nothing sexual, nothing overt, but I would memorize the silkiness of his skin, the feel of his chest, the strength of his arms, the odor between his legs when he would wrap them around my head and squeeze.

I put the car back in gear and turned it around.

The reunion was in the town park, next to the old, abandoned Carterville High School that closed in 1955 or so when the new consolidated high school opened. I was surprised to see the crumbling building was still standing after all this time. Wasn't it a health hazard or something? The school district had always been a poor one; there had never been the money to tear the old building down. All the old town high schools had been still there when I was in school.

Apparently, they all were still standing.

The parking area behind the crumbling old high school building was filled with cars. I glanced at my watch and saw I was about half an hour late. There was a keg of beer resting in a tin washtub underneath an old cottonwood tree; there was another washtub filled with soft drinks. Unlike previous reunions, which Jenna had told me about, there weren't any small kids running around, shrieking and screaming and playing. Of course not—this was the twenty-five-year reunion and my classmates' kids were too old by now to be dragged along. The cars, I noticed, were mostly pickup trucks and various other small cars that appeared to be inexpensive. I was right—the Mustang was a bit much. I maneuvered into a parking spot and shut off the engine. I lit a cigarette and watched the small groupings of people.

Would I even recognize anyone?

I got out of the car and ground out the cigarette under my shoe in the dirt. I hadn't seen any of these people in so many years. Did I even want to see any of them now? Why *had* I come?

I decided to get something to drink, and walked over to the washtubs. A taller bald man, maybe about twenty pounds overweight, was filling a plastic cup with beer from the keg. He was wearing a pair of faded jeans and a blue polo shirt. I stuck my hand into the icy water of the other tub and pulled out a can of Pepsi. When I popped the top he turned and looked at me. His face was deeply lined and tanned, and somewhat familiar.

"Dennis?" His eyes squinted at me.

My heart sank. Of all people to run into first! Steve Mallon. He'd been part of the in-crowd of jocks, and he'd never liked me much. He'd never been mean, but he'd rarely spoken to me, and usually had a scowl on his face when he did.

"Steve?" I asked.

He smiled. "It is you. Hear you've finally come out of the closet, huh?"

"Well, yeah."

He stuck out his hand. "Glad to hear it." I took his calloused hand and we shook. "There's nothin' worse than tryin' to be something you're not, is there?" He shook his head. "I knew when we were in school you were just pretendin'." He laughed. "Didn't know what you were pretendin', but I knew you weren't what you were pretendin' to be."

I laughed with him, loosening up a bit. "Yeah, well, I just tried to fit in."

"Couldn't have been easy." He took a swig out of his beer.

"Glad to hear that's all over and done with." He shrugged. "I just thought you were a phony in school, ya know? Didn't like it. Hear you're doing well for yourself."

"Yeah."

Jenna Bradley made her way over to us with a big grin on her face. Jenna had been a big girl in school; almost six feet tall and weighing in at well over two hundred pounds. She'd lost most of the weight but was still carrying some extra. Her brown hair was shot through with gray. There were lines on her face that didn't used to be there, dark circles under her eyes, and the skin on her neck was starting to sag just a little bit. She threw her arms around me. "You came!" she whispered into my ear. She stepped back a bit and winked at me. "You are looking good, Dennis!"

I grinned at her. "Thanks, Jenna. You look great too."

She ran a hand through her hair. "You really think so? Hell, I'm just an old broad now. Got a daughter starting college this fall, can you believe it?" She shook her head. "Where did all the time go?"

This didn't seem to need an answer, so I let her tuck her arm through mine and lead me into the groups of people. They were all at least polite to me, some of them friendly. I got hugs from women and handshakes from the men. I met husbands and wives I'd never known or just didn't remember. My classmates had, of course, all aged, and I thought I'd prepared myself for it. Doug Jennings, who'd been whip thin in school, still had skinny legs but a big beer gut hanging over the waistband of his jeans. His blond frizzy hair was long gone. Homecoming Queen Brenda Littrell had gained at least forty pounds, wore too much makeup, and her shellacked helmet of black hair was obviously dyed. Craig Jackson, my second biggest crush after Tony, who'd been blond and blue-eyed and had no body fat, had gone gray, his hairline had receded, and his body was fleshy and a little bloated. I looked at pictures of kids, made the necessary small talk, and laughed. But nobody asked me about my life; nobody asked about my other half back home, nobody asked about my career or my adventures. It was all casual small talk, the kind you share with people you might have once had something in common with, but time had turned into strangers.

After about half an hour of this I headed back to the parking lot to just breathe. I lit a cigarette and leaned against the Mustang. The reminiscing was starting now, the talk about why we lost that football game against Valley Falls, what happened the night of the prom, what happened at the hayride, and on and on. I had my own memories of those events, memories I didn't want to share despite their casual acceptance of me. I didn't want to share how I spent prom night watching Tony and wishing I could dance with him. I didn't want to share I'd watched Craig Jackson moon a truck driving by during the hayride and had stared, spellbound, at his perfectly shaped ass glowing in the moonlight. I was still on the outside with these people, and always would be. They had their memories and the similar paths their lives had taken since graduation; marriages, kids, worries about buying a house and money.

I leaned against the car smoking, wishing I had a joint.

A car pulled in and I didn't turn to see who it was. I wouldn't recognize the person anyway. The shock of connecting familiar names with unfamiliar faces had worn off, and I was getting a little tired of it all. I wondered how long it would be before I could safely beg off and head back for the hotel in Kahola.

"Dennis?"

I knew the voice. I would know that voice anywhere. I turned, and there he was. Tony Williams. "Tony?" I replied, my voice croaking just a little bit.

The face I'd loved so desperately in high school was the same, just some added wrinkles. The dark circles he'd always had under his blue eyes were still there, now deeper and darker. His thick black hair was cropped short close to his scalp. The big, muscular arms I remembered were thicker and sticking out of a red T-shirt with the sleeves cut off. His jeans were tight and his waist a little thicker than I remembered, but he looked so much the same.

For a brief second I wondered if his underwear was blue with red trim.

He held out his hand and we shook. He was smiling. "Wondered if you would make it this time."

I shrugged. "Yeah, well."

He leaned back against the car with me, the car dropping a bit under the added weight. "Jenna says you're doing well."

"Yeah."

He looked at the park, the small crowd of people. "Every time I come to one of these things I always wonder why I bother. They haven't changed since school."

There was a moment of silence. I didn't know what to say to him. What do you say to someone who was your first real love after twenty-five years of nothing but silence? I knew he was on his second marriage. I knew he had three kids. I knew he was a garbage man in Topeka.

Everything else was a mystery.

He pulled a joint out of his jeans pocket and lit it. He offered it to me, and I took a couple of drags. It wasn't the best pot I've ever had. It was strong and acrid, and I choked a bit, coughing. I took a quick swig of my Pepsi after handing it back to him. He grinned, the same devilish grin he had all those years ago, his eyes sparkling, the crooked grin that always made me weak, made me want to kiss him. "I can't ever handle these people without being stoned."

I laughed. I was feeling a little bit of a buzz. "I wish I would have brought some."

"Anybody call you a fag?"

"No." I shrugged. "They've all been nice, but phony nice, I guess. They don't know what to say to me, what to ask me, so they all just tell me what they've been up to." I looked at him. "You didn't bring your wife?"

"We're getting divorced." He handed the joint back to me. "Happily ever after doesn't seem to be in the cards for me."

"Sorry to hear that."

"Don't be."

We smoked in silence for a little while, until the joint was just a small roach, which he pinched out and put into his wallet. "So what do you think of the Class of 1978?"

"Things haven't changed much, I guess." I sighed. "I was an outsider then, I'm an outsider now. I'm not sure why I came, to tell the truth." I wasn't going to tell him I'd come to see him. I'd wanted to see him, to put to rest all the fantasies I'd had for the twenty-five years. Now that he was here and we were sitting with only a few scant inches between our bodies, I was reacting the way I always had. Glancing at him sideways out of the corner of my eyes, drinking in his muscular arms, the big chest wrapped tightly inside the red T-shirt, the strong legs in the tight jeans.

I still wanted him.

He laughed. "Well, you're the one who's changed, Mr. Big Shot Photographer. Out of the closet, living a high life, traveling the world, meeting famous people. I knew you were destined for something different than the rest of us." He looked at me. "You got out, but you weren't from here to begin with. You weren't tied to this fucking place." He shrugged. "I wanted out of here so bad, and yet here I am, twenty-five years later, still stuck in Kansas. I knew you'd get out." He laughed. "Man, I wanted to go with you."

I stared at him. "You did?"

"Yeah." He looked down at his shoes. "Part of the reason I liked you so much was because I wanted to get out of here, and I just knew you weren't going to stay. I kind of hoped you'd take me with you." He looked over at me. "Remember the night we camped out in your backyard?"

I'd forgotten about that night. We'd put up a tent and wrapped sleeping bags around us. We stayed up and watched the night sky, and talked until the sun started coming up in the distant east, its rays turning the night sky into beautiful combinations of navy blue, pinks, and oranges.

"You told me that night that every star was a promise, remember?"

"I did?"

He laughed. "Funny you don't remember; I've never forgotten. You said that every star was a promise, and the promises in every star were the kind that could never be broken."

*Kind of poetic for a seventeen-year-old*, I thought. "I said that?"

He nodded. "And we promised on a star, remember? We promised that we would always be friends, we would always be a part of each other's lives."

I did remember now, the two of us holding hands solemnly as we picked out a star and made our promise. And after we made the promise, we had hugged tightly, holding on to each other, our bare chests pressed hard against each other, and my dick had gotten hard. That spoiled the moment for me, and I had pulled back away from him, afraid he'd see it, afraid of the contempt I'd see in his face. "Yes, I remember that." My

heart ached for the seventeen-year-old I'd been, so desperate
for love, so desperate to belong somewhere, so desperately
afraid of who I really was.

"When you left I wished I'd said something, asked to go
with." Tony smiled.

"But I went away for college," I replied. "You couldn't
have come with me."

"Sure I could have." He shrugged. "I wouldn't have been
able to go to college, but we could have gotten an apartment
together off campus, and I could have gotten a job, and then
when you graduated, we could have moved to the big city
together."

"I don't think that would have been a good idea." I pictured
it. It would have been torture for me, seeing him every day in
his underwear around the house, trying to sneak glances at
him while he showered. The torture would have become even
worse when he brought girls home to fuck in his room, having
to listen to them fucking through his bedroom door but not
able to resist, always terrified of being caught.

"Why? Because you were in love with me?"

"You knew?" There was no point in denying it. Apparently
my acting in high school was not the Academy Award caliber
I had always believed it to be. What was the harm in admitting
to it at this point anyway?

"I always wondered what would have happened if you'd
ever tried anything." He gave me a quick glance, and just as
quickly glanced away.

"You'd have kicked my ass and told everyone at school."

"That's what you thought? No wonder you never tried
anything."

I lit a cigarette. "Believe me, I wanted to." I blew out a
plume of smoke. "But you never gave me any indication and

I wasn't about to initiate it." I could remember the fears that took years to get past.

Even after I had come out, how long had it been before I had the courage to approach another man in a bar?

He grinned at me. "What about our wrestling?"

"What about it?"

"I always got hard." He shrugged. "I always kinda thought that it might lead somewhere. But it never did."

"I guess we were both afraid."

"Yeah." He playfully punched me in the arm. "I guess we were both a pair of pussies."

I laughed. No one had referred to me as a "pussy" since my fraternity days. "Yeah, I guess."

"What are you doing later on tonight?"

*Is he asking me for a date, for Christ's sake?* I stared at him. "My flight back isn't until tomorrow, so I'm staying at the Best Western in Kahola tonight."

"After this is over I have to go see my mom." He shrugged. "I can grab a pizza and a six-pack and come by, if you want."

"Yeah," I said softly. "I want."

The rest of the afternoon passed by in a blur. I talked to some people, made some lame jokes, laughed. Some of my classmates got drunk off the keg beer. Mine kept getting warm since I wasn't drinking it fast enough and had to keep pouring it out into the grass. My senior prom date, Lisette Kidwell Armitage, clung to my arm for over half an hour, bitching about her husband and how sorry she was she never got out of Kansas. What could I say to that? I just smiled and nodded, looking for rescue from any quarter. She stank of beer and sweat, her fine blond bangs plastered to her forehead with perspiration. There was dirt beneath her bitten fingernails. I finally escaped, pawning her off on Clay Perkins, her homecoming date. Clay had never liked me in school, had once called me a "fag" at football practice. *Tit for tat*, I thought, *here ya go, breeder, you deal with her.* I smiled and excused myself. The party was breaking up; before I could make my escape I had to pose for pictures with so many people I barely remembered, and the obligatory photo of the class. Tony knelt beside me in the front in the grass.

"You getting out of here?" he whispered to me.

"Soon as the picture's taken."

"I'll see you in a few hours, then," he said, and winked at me.

I made my good-byes, gave my address to a few people I'd never hear from again, gave Jenna a big hug and a kiss, and got in the Mustang. Fleetwood Mac roared from the stereo as I drove out of the lot with a sigh of relief.

I'd never see any of them ever again, I thought as I made the turn onto the Carterville Road, heading back to Kahola.

My stomach was growling, so I made my way up Sixth Street and hit the drive-thru at the McDonald's. It amazed me it was still there, but so little in Kahola had changed. The sweet smell from the Dolly Madison plant when I'd crossed the highway into town. The stink of slaughtered beef and sour blood from the meat packing plant on the other side of town when I'd made the turn onto Sixth Street. When I turned into the drive-thru, I felt as though I'd driven back in time for the second time that day.

I'd worked at that McDonald's my senior year as a show of independence, flipping burgers and getting the stink of grease into my hair and my pores. The girl working the drive-thru window was maybe seventeen, with her blond hair pulled back under her cap and a sprinkle of pimples across her young cheeks. She smiled and took my money, handed me the sack with my Quarter Pounder with cheese, gave me my change, and thanked me for stopping at McDonald's and asked me to stop by again. I just smiled at her, looking beyond her at the other kids in the ugly brown polyester uniforms moving about, grabbing burgers and bags of fries, pouring drinks. I saw myself, fresh-faced, so heartbreakingly young, feathered brown bangs sweeping back from my face, smiling and joking with the other kids, squirting ketchup and mustard onto toasted buns, two pickles on each one, a handful of onions followed by yellow cheese, sweat running down my cheeks. I ate the Quarter Pounder as I drove back up Prairie Street, where the Best Western was perched on a slow-rising hill overlooking the highway to Kansas City. I crumpled up the wrapper, placed it in the bag and threw it into the backseat. I stopped at the Coke machine and got myself a can.

I showered, washing off the sweat and memories. I put on a clean pair of white 2(x)ist underwear, a pair of white cotton shorts, and a red tank top. I flipped through the meager lineup of cable channels provided, finally settling in to watch a really bad Joan Crawford movie, *Berserk*, on what was supposedly a "classic" movie channel.

Apparently I fell asleep after a few minutes, because when the knocking on my door started I sat up, disoriented. The digital clock on the nightstand read 6:07. I wiped my eyes and walked across the darkened room to the door. I flipped on the light switch next to the door before opening it.

Tony smiled at me. In one hand he held a Pizza Hut box, in the other a plastic grocery store bag with a six-pack of Coors Light tall boys perspiring in the late afternoon heat. "Hope you still like pepperoni and sausage."

"Come on in." I stood aside and let him pass. He set the pizza and beer down on the little round table right next to the air-conditioning unit and flipped the box top open. The room filled with the smell of cooked meats and melted cheese. Lazy tendrils of steam rose. He popped the top on one of the beers and took a swig.

I sat down and took a beer. We talked while we ate the pizza and drank the beers, small talk that revealed nothing about either one of us, like we were two strangers making conversation. We talked about the Kansas City Royals, about how Kansas State had finally managed to turn its long-suffering football team around into a championship contender year in, year out, about our classmates and how badly most of them had aged. He didn't ask me about my life and I didn't ask him about his, as though by mutual unspoken agreement the topic was off-limits. I wanted to ask about his two wives, about his kids. I wanted to ask about his curiosity about sex with another man, if it was something he'd always felt and just never acted on.

Finally, all that was left of the pizza were some gnawed-on crusts in a greasy cardboard box.

He popped the lid on another beer. "You remember Rob Hinton?"

"Yeah." Rob Hinton had been a year behind us in school. He had a good body, I remembered, a nice round hard ass with very pale skin, blue eyes, and light brown hair. Rob and I had been friends at first, but when I was a senior that changed. I never really knew why. "How's he doing?"

"He died in a car accident a few years ago. Driving drunk." Tony settled back into his chair and crossed his right leg over his left. "Left a wife and three kids."

"That's too bad." I shrugged.

"You know he used to—" He looked away from me. "When we were in school—"

"What?"

"Aw, hell, it doesn't matter anymore." He looked me square in the eye. "Rob and I used to mess around some."

"Really?"

"Yeah. I mean, we never fucked or anything like that, but we used to beat each other off sometimes."

I laughed. "What a pair of fags."

He put his hand on my knee. It was damp. "I always wondered what it would be like, you know? To be with another guy. *Really* be with another guy."

I stood up and pulled my tank top over my head. He did the same, and we stood there, facing each other, scant inches apart, shirtless, both of us breathing harder than we had been just the moment before, and I leaned in toward him and put my mouth on his.

It wasn't the way I fantasized it would be all those years ago. Back then, I imagined our mouths coming together in a frenzy, all tongues and lips weaving in and around each other, pulling each other closer in a mad explosion of passion and lust. This kiss was soft, and gentle, our lips touching, our bodies still apart, not touching each other anywhere except at the lips. He tasted of stale smoke, beer, and slightly of pizza and garlic. His lips were soft. I reached out with my right hand and placed it on his hard chest, touching his nipple, which hardened under my fingers.

I pulled my head back. He opened his eyes, those brilliant blue eyes, and smiled at me. "That's nice."

I took his hand and led him to the bed. We stood there, looking at each other, my body starting to respond to his. His chest was still big and muscular, but his stomach wasn't flat anymore, just a little bit of a paunch, with the wiry black hairs around his navel trailing down to the waist of his shorts. He reached and undid mine, and I let them fall, stepping out of them. He pushed me gently and I fell back onto the bed, and he took off his shorts, standing there in a pair of white BVDs that had been washed many many times, more grayish than white now, and he lay down beside me. Our arms went around each other and we kissed again, this time deeper, more passionately, and I could feel his own erection through the frail cotton of his underwear.

It wasn't like I thought it would be, all those times as I lay in my bed with my eyes closed and my underwear bunched around my ankles, it wasn't fire and music and fireworks going off. It was unsure, tender, maybe a little on the sweet side, as our mouths and hands explored each other uncertainly. And when I finally entered him, and he was able to relax enough to take me inside, a single tear rolled out of his left eye. I watched the tear trace its way down his cheek, his eyes closed, as I slowly made my way into him and wondered what the tear was for—was it sadness at releasing himself so completely to me, was it for time lost? There was just that single tear, alone and orphaned, but his eyes remained closed as I worked, gently and steadily, to bring us both to the climax we had waited so many years to have together.

And when it was over, and I was handing him a towel to wipe himself down with, I lit a cigarette. "Was it what you were expecting?" I asked finally. Tomorrow, I would be on a plane back to my life, to my world, to my partner. Tonight Tony would be driving back to Topeka and his life as a sanitation worker, with his soon-to-be-divorced second wife and kids.

"It hurt a little bit, but it also felt good." He didn't look at me. He slipped his underwear back on, pulled his tank top over his head. "I, um, I really have to get going."

I smiled. How many times had I heard that before in my life? How many times had I said it to someone? I blew smoke at the ceiling. "Long drive back to Topeka."

He buckled his shorts and tied his shoelaces. "Yeah." He walked over to the door.

I got off the bed and walked over to the door naked. "Good-bye, Tony."

He looked at me and smiled, a sad sort of smile that didn't quite reach his eyes. "What might have been, huh?" He touched my cheek with his right hand, rubbing it gently. "It was good seeing you."

"Likewise."

The door shut behind him. I stood there for a moment and remembered two teenaged boys, sitting out underneath the stars in their sleeping bags, their hands locked together in a fierce grip, their futures uncertain but with a wealth of so many possibilities. I saw us again sitting together on the bus coming back from an away football game, laughing and teasing with the other guys on the team. I remembered studying for a history test, asking him questions and having to give him the answers. I pulled my shorts on and walked outside, to the little balcony off my room. I saw him down in the parking lot getting into his car. He looked up at me, and smiled, and gave me a little wave. I waved back.

The sun had gone down and the sky was cobalt, sprinkled with tiny little pinpoints of light that winked and blinked.

I looked up at them for a moment, and back down as his car drove out of the parking lot.

"There are still promises in every star, Tony," I said, flicking my cigarette ash over the balcony's edge. I brushed a tear out of my eye. "They're just made to other people now."

And I went back inside.

## Tell Me a Lie

The music is loud, almost at eardrum-bleeding levels, so loud it's almost impossible to think about anything on a level higher than instinctual. With the music so loud the walls are even vibrating, it's difficult to think about anyone as more than just a piece of meat, a body to stroke and caress and fuck. A thin veil of smoke hovers a few feet over the heads of the chattering, drinking patrons. A group of pretty young men who look barely out of their teens toss back shots and choke a bit before laughing and grinning and pounding each other on the back, proud of their rapid descent into alcoholic stupor. The dance floor isn't crowded—too early for that—but there are some guys out there moving mindlessly to the driving beat of the music. One has his shirt off and tucked into the back of his low-rise jeans, a rippled torso glistening in the lights flashing off the mirror ball over his head. A tanned, thickly muscled man wearing a pair of boots and a red bikini shakes his ass on the opposite side of the bar from me, coaxing dollar bills from a gaggle of older men gathered at his feet, staring up with their mouths open.

I watch him for a moment. It is truly a wondrous ass, thick and muscular, and perched atop two well-defined, strong legs. I cannot help but smile as I stare at his ass as he moves it from side to side, but not in beat with the music. There is a tattoo on his lower back just above the red stretch fabric, but in the glow of the black lights I can't make out what it is. It doesn't matter. He's a terrible dancer, probably gay for pay like so many of them are, and who has time for that kind of nonsense? The body is remarkable, but there are a lot of guys in the place just as hot as he who won't require cash up front for a fuck. Not that I have anything against paying for sex, of course, but I'm just not at the point where I can't get it for free anymore.

*Maybe I should have just stayed home and gone online,* I think to myself again. *I've been here for almost an hour and no one's even looked at me twice—but then again, there isn't anyone here besides the stupid dancer I'd even talk to, let alone fuck. And the more I drink, the lower my standards will go.* How many times has that happened to me? I shudder to think. I look at my watch. *Another half hour and I'm out of here,* I decide. Home to my empty apartment and the glow of the computer screen as I cruise manhunt.com and hope someone even halfway decent messages me. But I don't want that again, the wait for them to knock on my door and the enormous disappointment when I see their picture was at least ten years out of date, or they haven't been to the gym in a couple of years, or any number of things…that's why I prefer going to bars to find someone. At least in a bar you can see what you're getting (as long as you stay reasonably sober) and you don't have to experience that awkward moment when he is standing on your doorstep and you have to resist the urge to slam the door in his face, that horrible split second of resignation of *a live body's better than jacking off alone to porn again.*

I sip my beer and see a guy walk around the corner. I've seen him before, over the years. Desire rises in my heart and groin. I've always wanted him, but he was always with another guy who always seemed to stick protectively close to him—

or been part of a group with no apparent interest in hooking up with anyone. He's beautiful. He's about six feet tall or thereabouts, with dark hair he cuts short and hides beneath a baseball cap—tonight it's an LSU cap. He has the thickly muscled body of a football player, and always wears T-shirts and tight jeans. Tonight is no exception. His face is gorgeous, with wide blue eyes and tanned skin—there's probably some Cajun in his background. I've cruised the contact sites looking for him before, with no luck. He's either faceless in his profiles or just not online looking for Mr. Right Now. I watch as he walks up to the bar directly across from me, ignoring the stripper gyrating near where he is standing.

Our eyes meet, and he smiles at me. He has a beautiful smile, the kind I'd like to see in the morning when I wake him with a kiss on the neck. His right eye closes in a wink before he breaks contact.

*Is he interested?* I wonder as I set my beer back down on the bar. Or was it just random chance that our eyes met as we both cruised? Should I look back over? What if it was just an accident?

Play it cool.

Don't act too eager.

That's always a mistake.

I finish my beer and order another. I look over out of the corner of my eye. He's still there. He's looking the other way, his back to me, facing the dance floor watching the guy without a shirt. I look back at the guy he's watching. He's dancing by himself, and has been for about an hour. He's rolling, high on something, and every once in a while he misses the beat and stumbles a bit. But he's sexy. His jeans are riding low, and as he dances around again I can see the slight curve to his upper buttocks, a hint of the crack of his ass. Damn. I look back at the guy I've zeroed in on, willing him to turn back toward me.

*Come on, look back at me, you don't want that drugged-out loser. Sure he's hot, but he probably can't get hard. I can.* I keep looking, willing him to move his eyes back over here. *Come on, baby.* Just when I think the telepathy isn't working…he turns around back to the bar.

And turns his head in my direction.

Our eyes meet again.

I smile, and move my head down in a slow, shy movement. Like I'm embarrassed to be caught looking. It's a trick I've perfected over the years. The shy grin, the down-turned head—it almost never fails. It gives off a vibe that most guys can't resist, the notion they are so hot I don't consider myself worthy of their incredible beauty. *Who, me? You're looking at ME?*

There aren't many gay men who can pass up that kind of flattery. I follow up with a shy glance back in his direction and I smile to myself as I turn my back to the bar and lean back against it. He's walking this way. Pay dirt.

Let the games begin.

"Hey," he says, standing right in front of me, his legs slightly spread apart, smiling at me. His teeth are white and even. At this close range I can smell his musk. My dick gets a little harder in my jeans. "How's it going?"

"Okay," I say back, allowing my own smile to creep across my face. I keep my head tilted down at a slight angle, once again to give the impression of shyness.

"Where are you from?" he says. It's the typical New Orleans opening line—everyone uses it, it seems. Well, it may not be original, but I've left with people with more inane opening lines before. "I don't think I've ever seen you before."

That, of course, is a lie. But I let it pass. When I was younger and more foolish, I used to correct guys when they tried that gambit. "Oh, I'm from here. Where are you from?" This time I look him in the eyes and smile as wide as I can. I have a great smile. It's very hard to resist.

"Oh, I live here too. Why haven't I seen you before?" His own smile widens, dimples sinking into his cheeks. My God, he's fucking adorable.

I resist the urge to laugh. "I don't get out much." I can lie just as easily as anyone else. And part of this whole bar ritual, the mating dance of the modern gay man, requires *some* lying. Honesty will almost always chase away your catch, and I need him too much. If I lose and he walks away—it is home to the computer, and I don't want that. He's my last chance tonight in this bar, and I've already invested several hours and spent fifteen bucks on beer in this place. I am not going home empty-handed. Does it matter that I've seen him before? No, it doesn't. This is just the first time we've spoken—so therefore it is the first time I've existed in his world, and that's just fine with me. I don't want a lover. I don't want a boyfriend. I don't want a date. I want to fuck, and he is hot as hell and I want him. I want to feel his arms around me. I want my cock in his beautiful ass. I want to make him moan and scream and shoot buckets of come out of his cock.

But *is* he interested? I hate this early part of the dance. Maybe he's just bored, passing some time until his friends get here. I've never seen him alone before, but I can't ask him about it; I've already implied I've never seen him before. I steal a glance down at the crotch of his tight jeans. He doesn't appear to have a hard-on, but sometimes it's hard to tell— especially if they are wearing boxer shorts. But at least he isn't wearing those stupid fucking baggy jeans so many guys are wearing these days. Those are the worst. Those make everyone look hung like a horse—and the majority of them *definitely* are not. Most are disappointing once their clothes come off.

Isn't that the worst, when you get a guy home and his clothes off and you realize there's nothing more than a hypodermic needle down there and scrawny white chicken legs and an ass that sags ever so slightly but it's still noticeable—

And *that's* the trouble with baggy jeans.

But he's wearing tight jeans that hug his strong, thick legs. No, there won't be much disappointment on that score when I peel him out of them.

"I'm Troy, by the way." He sticks his hand out. I shake it. His hand is big and his grip strong. I feel an electric jolt that goes right to my cock. I wonder if he felt it too.

"Phil," I say, wondering if his name is really Troy. I seem to recall being told on another night by someone that his name was Ken, but it doesn't really matter. I don't want to marry him.

I don't even want his phone number.

"Nice to meet you." He gives me an even deeper smile. The dimples flash at me again. He really is quite beautiful.

"Back atcha." I smile back at him.

What to talk about now? The weather? *Want to come home and fuck me till I can't walk? Is that a cucumber in your pocket or a roll of Life Savers? Can we go into the bathroom and piss so we can sneak peeks at each other to see if we both measure up?* Wouldn't that be better than wasting time on idle chatter? Wouldn't it be more honest? The bathhouse is more honest. There, no one pretends you're anything more than just a fuck. No names. Anonymous. Just get off and be on your way. It's a hell of a lot more honest than this bar bullshit. But I'm not in the mood to go to the bathhouse. And I've reeled this one in already. Now I have to come up with something to keep the conversation going, to keep things rolling, before he loses interest and throws me back.

It would be so much more honest to say, "Hey, are you as

horny as I am? I live a block away—want to come home with me?"

But you can't play the game that way. It doesn't work. I've tried it before. You have to pretend at first that neither of you are horny. You have to pretend this might be the start of the relationship you've always dreamed of, even though you know damned well it's not. It's just a trick, but I don't want to scare him off with honesty.

I'm tired of being alone. I don't want to be lonely tonight. He's good-looking enough. His body is hot as fuck. He definitely works out—*wait a minute, there you go!*

"Where do you work out?" I ask, sipping on my beer. "You look like you work out all the time."

He laughs, pleased. "Hardly. I'm lucky if I get in there three times a week. I work out at Elmwood in Harahan."

Harahan? Interesting. Not an Orleans Parish boy. Definitely will be heading back to my place, if all goes according to plan—I am not going all the way out there and having to drive back to the Quarter. I finish my beer and toss the empty into a trash can. "What's your secret?" I ask, tentatively reaching out and brushing my hand on his chest. "I'd love to get my chest that size."

He laughs again. "I don't know. You look pretty hot yourself. You need another beer?"

"Thanks."

He orders and pays for it, passing it to me. "You want to go out on the balcony?"

"Sure."

We step out into the warm night air. The balcony isn't crowded, and we lean over the iron railing and look down onto St. Ann Street. He stands next to me. Very close. His arm is hard muscle. I like the way it feels against mine. I almost start purring. I sip my beer. "Nice night," I say.

He kisses my ear.

He's moving faster than I thought he would, but that's not a bad thing. His breath against my ear raises goose bumps on my arm. I moan a bit, quietly, but loud enough for him to hear. I feel one of his hands brush against my ass, and I lean into him. He's warm.

"You're beautiful," he whispers.

I let out a shy giggle and look downward. It's automatic. Don't even have to think about that one. There's a group of pretty boys without shirts on in the street below. Yum. I'd like to dive into that covered in baby oil...

He moves a little until he's behind me. His arms go around my waist. He kisses my neck, quick little butterfly kisses that make me close my eyes and shiver a little. His chest is pressed up against my back. It's hard. Granite. Marble. Rock. I lean back into him. My butt brushes up against his crotch. I can feel it stirring, but unless it's erect there's still no telling how big he is. I debate pushing my ass against him, but change my mind. That will come in due time, but right now I can't seem too easy, too ready to just take him home and let him fuck me. I assume he's a top from the way he wants to be behind me, and as I think it his crotch rubs against my ass again.

Now he's hard.

And it *is* a big one.

I resist the urge to turn around and suck him off right there.

Desire is overcoming good sense. I turn around and put my arms around him and press my mouth against his. He kisses me back, and my lips part as I start sucking on his tongue. His eyes close as we work our bodies against each other.

I want him to come home with me. No more playing the game, no more coquettish bar antics.

In my mind I can see him in my bed, naked, his big cock hard as he smiles at me.

I pull back from him a little bit, and we smile at each other.

"Wow," he whispers.

"Yeah."

"Where do you live?"

I swallow. "Around the corner."

"You want to go there?"

I nod and he kisses me again. He takes me by the hand and we walk through the bar, down the staircase and out the door onto the sidewalk. I lead him down to Dauphine Street and the front door of my place. My hands are shaking a bit as I try to fit the key into the lock. But somehow I manage to get the door open, and we are standing in my living room, our arms around each other, hands groping and fondling as we kiss again, deep and wet and hard, and my cock is hard, and I can feel his hardness through his jeans…and then he pulls my shirt over my head and starts sucking on my right nipple.

I moan.

It is so intense my body starts to tremble as his tongue, lips, and teeth work my nipple. And his hands are undoing my pants, yanking them down, and his mouth is on my cock, sucking and licking and moving on it. He is a master at cocksucking, and all I can think as he works my cock with his mouth is how horny I am, how turned on I am, how badly I want him inside me, and then…

And I place my hands on his head. "Stop, I'm going to come."

He ignores me and pushes my hands away. He keeps working and there's nothing I can do, my entire body goes rigid and he pulls his mouth away just as I start to come, my load is shooting out of my convulsing body onto the hardwood floors. And when I am finished, I stand there, my pants down around my ankles. "Wow," I say finally.

"Yeah." He smiles back at me, and stands up. He glances at his watch. "Thanks, man, nothing I love more than sucking a cock."

"Thank you," I reply.

He moves over to the front door. "Catch ya later." And before I can say another word, the door is shutting behind him.

Gone.

The house is silent.

It takes a few moments for the reality to sink in.

The clock on the mantel strikes midnight.

And I am alone again.

I pull my pants back up.

*That was honest,* I think as I turn the television on.

A small part of me wishes he'd asked for my phone number.

I sit down on the couch and start flipping through the channels.

## ALL THE WORLD'S A STAGE

The dance floor was still crowded with shirtless boys, sweat running down smooth muscled torsos. My friends had moved on across the street to Oz, leaving me alone on the dance floor enjoying my Ecstasy high and the charms of a guy in his late twenties with the body of an underwear model and the face of an angel. His ass was round and hard in his jeans, and he kept grinding it into my crotch with the beat of the music. He had a tattoo on his lower back, a black and gold fleur-de-lis, the emblem of the New Orleans Saints. Every time he would back into me that way, my dick would get hard in my jean shorts. I wasn't sure if he actually wanted me to fuck him or not. You never can be sure of anything at a circuit party. His flirting could be entirely based in whatever mind-altering substance he'd imbibed. He was riding on the dance floor, just flirting, getting attention from men he found hot. It was flattering, for sure, since I am now in my late forties, and I had always been brainwashed into thinking that gay life—and most assuredly gay sex and desire—ended at forty.

And if this boy fucked the way he danced, well, it would definitely be worth my while.

He backed into me again, and I slid my arms around his waist, pulling him back against me. His body was wet with sweat, his jeans damp to the touch, his short blond hair glistening in the flickering laser lights. My cock hardened again, and I ground my crotch into the back of his jeans, rubbing it against him. He spun around suddenly, so our crotches were together. I could feel his hard-on against mine. He pressed his lips against mine, forcing mine apart with his tongue. I sucked on his tongue when it entered my mouth, reaching down to cup that pretty ass with my hands.

"Mmmmmm." He smiled as he pulled his head back from mine. He put both of his hands on my pectoral muscles, squeezing a little bit. "Very nice."

I smiled back at him. "I could say the same."

He bent down and started licking my right nipple just as another wave of the drug swept over me. My head went back, lost in the pleasure his tongue was sending through me, the drug heightening my own awareness. My cock was hard, my balls starting to hurt just a little bit, needing release soon. His hand went down to my crotch, sliding inside the waistband of my shorts and cradling my aching cock.

He stopped working my nipple and grinned at me, squeezing my cock again. "That's really nice—bet that would feel really good inside me."

I wanted him. I squeezed his ass again. "That feels hot."

"You like to eat ass?" He was still holding my cock. "I love to have my ass eaten. It fucking drives me insane."

"I could eat your ass for hours."

He kissed me again. "Baby, I'll hold you to that." He kissed my neck and pulled me closer to him so we were standing pressed together almost from head to toe, swaying to the music. The music began to slow a bit, and the lights on the dance floor began to come up again. I noticed security guys clearing the stage a few feet from where we were dancing. He stepped back from me for a moment. He got a puzzled look on his face. "How old are you?" he asked, staring at my face.

The music continued to get lower. "Forty-seven."

His eyes got round. "Wow. My dad is forty-five."

The music stopped.

I stood there staring at him.

He smiled back at me.

A huge drag queen climbed up on the stage. "Hello, New Orleans!" she said into a microphone, and the crowd on the dance floor shouted back at her. She was wearing all black, with a huge blond wig towering at least a foot over her face. She had to weigh at the very least two hundred and fifty pounds, but like all large drag queens, she was fabulous. Her makeup, despite the steamy heat, was flawless. Her fingernails were long and red, the heels on her shoes stilettos. *How does she manage them at her size*, I wondered crazily. "I'm Kiki Van Diver, and do we have a show for you tonight!"

I'd never seen Kiki Van Diver in person before. She was one of the great auteurs of gay porn video. I kept staring at her.

It was easier to focus on her than to think about what this boy had just said.

The concept that I was older than his father was too much for me to handle.

Don't think about it.

Don't think about the fact you were sucking cock before he was born.

Don't think about the fact you are twice his age.

Just don't think about it.

He pressed up against me again. "Will you call me boy while you fuck me?"

Don't think about it.

My hard-on was gone.

Two guys wearing leather jocks and masks climbed up on the stage with Kiki. "I've brought two of my biggest stars with me," Kiki said into the microphone, and the crowd cheered again. They stood on either side of her. "This is Chad Morehead." She stroked the perfectly chiseled smooth chest of the guy on her right. "Isn't he pretty?" The crowd roared its approval. "He's a top and he's got a great big old dick, don't you, Chad?" In answer, he reached down and gripped it. It was huge, at least eleven inches long and about eight inches around.

"Wow," the boy said.

Damn it, don't think of him as a boy.

"And this," Kiki turned to the other guy, who was shorter and more thickly muscled than Chad, "is Cody Laws. Cody likes to get fucked, don't you, Cody?"

He answered her by turning around and showing a round, hard, muscled butt that could probably crack walnuts. He wiggled it at the audience.

"Any tops out there?" Kiki asked. There was some applause. "I bet someone out there would love to fuck this tight ass." She smacked it for emphasis.

Music started playing. Chad and Cody started dancing, moving toward each other. Chad reached out and grabbed Cody's jock and pulled him closer with it. They started kissing, their bodies pressed up against each other, rubbing their crotches together.

"How'd you like to be the meat in that sandwich?" Kiki asked.

"Oh, man, do you think they'll fuck up there?" the boy whispered to me.

Chad tore Cody's jock off and threw it into the audience. Cody's thick cock sprang up, slapping against his abs. His pubic hair was perfectly trimmed into a little square. It was the only place besides his head where hair showed on his body. Chad forced him down to his knees, where Cody started licking Chad's cock through his jock.

Kiki walked down the steps at the side of the stage. "New Orleans has always been pretty good to me and my boys," she said, walking through the crowd, "and to thank you all for being such a great crowd in a great city, I'm going to pick someone out of this audience to join my boys up there." By now, Cody had torn off Chad's jock and was deep-throating Chad's enormous cock.

"Oh man, I hope she picks me," the boy said.

Kiki stopped right in front of us. "What do we have here?" She looked at the boy. "Very pretty." She tweaked one of his nipples.

"Hey." He practically was wiggling.

She looked at me.

"Would you take a look at this one?" She reached behind the boy and stroked my chest. "Hot, hot, hot."

I didn't say anything. A spotlight came on and focused on the two of us. The boy, looking a little hurt, stepped out of the circle of light.

I didn't know what to say.

"Who wants to see this hot man naked?"

The crowd cheered.

"Um, I don't think so," I said.

"Come on now, don't be shy." She grabbed my hand and started pulling me to the stage.

I started to resist, but caught a glimpse of the boy.

*You're older than my dad…*

What the hell, I thought, and stopped resisting.

I climbed the steps.

Chad and Cody separated, looking at me, sizing me up.

Kiki undid my shorts and yanked them down.

I wasn't wearing underwear.

The crowd cheered.

I stepped out of the shorts and stood there naked.

"What do you think, boys?"

Cody and Chad stood on either side of me.

"Top or bottom?" Chad whispered.

I touched his chest. His skin was soft over the hard muscle. My cock began to come to life again. "Top."

"Awesome." Cody grinned. He dropped to his knees and started sucking my dick.

He was very good at it.

Chad kissed me, turning me sideways so that we were both in profile to the audience. Cody was working both of our cocks as Chad and I kissed. I started pinching Chad's huge nipples. He smiled at me, then tilted his head back and moaned. I started kissing his neck. He kept moaning. Cody was licking my cock. His tongue felt great, damp and velvety as it slid over the head of my cock and then along the underside. He took both my balls in his mouth and began sucking.

Oh man.

Chad leaned down and began flicking my nipples with his tongue.

I began to tremble, goose bumps rising on my skin.

Cody moved up my torso with his mouth until he had his mouth on my right nipple while Chad was nibbling on the left. I slid my right hand down and slipped a finger into Cody's moist hole. He stiffened for a moment, then his whole body relaxed as I moved the finger around in a circle. He smiled up at me. "That's good, Sir, that's really good."

*Sir?*

"I wanna fuck you, boy." I growled at him, removing the finger and slapping his ass. It was hard as a rock, no give at all beneath the slap. I was vaguely aware of the crowd cheering as I kept smacking his ass.

Cody stood up and pushed Chad away from the two of us. He turned so his ass was facing me, and bent over at the waist. He pushed his ass against my cock. Chad stepped forward and started slapping Cody's face with his huge cock.

Kiki slipped a condom over my dick and squirted lube on it. "Fuck him hard, Daddy man," she said into the microphone, which set off another round of cheers from the crowd down below on the dance floor.

I slid my cock into his ass slowly. Nice and slow, waiting for him to relax and loosen up. When I was about halfway in, I stopped and rotated my hips in a circular motion. His body stiffened at first, and seemed to let go. He was sucking Chad's horse cock, taking it all the way down his throat. Chad grinned at me and reached over to pinch my nipples. I didn't move for a moment, enjoying the feel of Cody's moist hole on my dick while Chad tweaked and pulled on my nipples.

I began to slip my cock out, barely moving. When all that was left inside was the head, I stopped and stood there. I looked out at the sea of faces on the dance floor. They were all watching us, hypnotized. For just an instant, I looked for the boy, but couldn't pick his face out.

*If my coworkers could see me now*, I thought.

I shoved my cock all the way in, until my balls slapped against his ass. I stood there, grinding my cock in deeper and deeper until Cody went up on his toes. He had stopped sucking Chad, who was slapping his face again with his dick. Cody's entire body began to shake.

"Plow him hard, man," Chad said. "Fast deep and hard."

I grinned at him. "Works for me."

I started sliding back and forth, pulling all the way out

slowly, so Cody whimpered a little as his hole reluctantly let go. When all that was left in was the head, I paused before slamming deep and hard back into him. His ass felt great. Cody started sucking on Chad's cock again, timing it so when I was moving backward and out of him, Chad was sliding out of his mouth. The muscles in Cody's back flexed as I moved in and out of him, sweat glistening on the tanned skin. I grabbed onto his hips and started pounding, moving faster and faster—no more of that slow shit. He was still working Chad's cock with his mouth.

Someone in the crowd started chanting, "Go! Go! Go!" and everyone else started chanting as well.

*It's like sex as sport*, I thought momentarily as I could feel my balls starting to constrict, a crowd cheering us on as we worked toward our orgasm, an Olympics of sex and I was going for the gold.

Chad pulled away from Cody's mouth, saliva glistening on his dick as he pumped with both hands, his body stiffening as he started to come, thick drops of white spraying into Cody's face.

The crowd cheered and I felt my own starting, so I kept pounding, even though my lower back was starting to ache just a bit. Each thrust inside was now forcing a grunt out of Cody.

His ass tightened, gripping me like a vise as he screamed.

I went up on my toes as I came inside him.

Sweat ran into my eyes as Kiki handed me a towel with a big grin. I took off the condom and she knotted it, tossing it into a garbage can in front of the stage. I wiped my face and handed the towel to Cody. He was smiling, his eyes slightly glazed. He wiped Chad's come off his face and kissed me.

"Man, that was incredible."

"Thanks."

The lights dimmed and the music started blaring again.

I pulled my shorts back up. Kiki handed me a card. "If you ever want to do a video, call me." She kissed my cheek. "I'll make you a star."

"We're done here at five," Chad said, stroking my chest. "If you want to come back to our hotel room for a private session, be at the front door around five." He winked. "Hope you can make it."

I climbed down the steps and headed for the bar, ordering a bottled water.

The reality of what I had done began to hit me as guys started slapping me on the back, kissing me on the cheek, shouting things I couldn't understand over the music. I just smiled, took my water and walked out onto the balcony. There was a light drizzle, more of a mist actually, and I stood at the railing looking down at the crowd in the street.

"Hey."

I turned.

It was the boy.

He was smiling at me. "That was amazing."

"Thanks."

"Could you fuck me that way?"

I pulled him into me, my arms around him, and kissed him. "Yeah, I think that could be arranged."

## Angels Don't Fall in Love

A ngel…"
I wake up in the middle of the night whispering his name. When my alarm goes off at seven in the morning, for that brief instant I imagine that he is there with me in the bed, that he never left, that his warm body is lying there next to me, and when I open my eyes his round liquid brown eyes will be looking into mine with that curious sexy mixture of innocence and awareness. But my eyes open, as they do every morning, to see the other side of the bed empty, a vast desolate waste of cotton sheets and woolen blankets. My heart sinks again, down into that blackness, the darkness of despair, loneliness, and missed opportunity. For I have known love, I have known passion, I have known joy.

And lost it.

I first laid eyes on Angel one night wandering home from the bars at about two in the morning. I'd had more than my fair share of drinks that night, and was giving up and going home. Staying out didn't mean meeting the man of my dreams, or even just a warm body with a forgettable name for the night. It just meant more alcohol, more disappointment, standing alone in a corner of the bar, not approaching anyone, nobody approaching me. Before going out that night I'd made a promise to myself that I would break the cycle. I would not stay out ordering more drinks thinking that maybe in five minutes the right guy would walk in. The drinks would only cloud my judgment and distort the way guys looked, making them look far better than they would in the cold light of morning, when I would ask myself, what were you thinking? It was a tired old game, and one I didn't feel like playing anymore.

He was standing, leaning against a lamppost on Royal Street just a block from my apartment. He was smoking a cigarette dangling from his lower lip. His hair was that dark shade of black that looks blue in the light. There was a mustache and goatee, and he was wearing one of those white ribbed tank tops that cling. His jeans were several sizes too big and were slung low across his hips, exposing black boxer shorts. There was a tattoo on his right arm, a cross in outline with beams of light radiating from it. In the flickering light of the gaslit lamp he seemed to be a large presence, but when I got closer I saw that he was maybe five-five, five-six possibly. His eyes were amazing, round liquid pools of brown with golden flecks in them, like the sad eyes of a Madonna in a Renaissance painting by a forgotten master. They were framed by long, curling lashes that looked dewy in the light.

"Hey." He nodded as I started to walk past him.

"Hey." I nodded, but stopped walking when I saw him cast his eyes down at the cracked and tilted sidewalk, but a shy smile starting to spread across his face. The smile ignited the lights behind his eyes; he seemed to radiate light and purity. "How ya doing?"

He shrugged, the smile staying in place. "On my last cigarette." He took one last drag and tossed it into the street.

"Drag."

"Ain't it, though?"

I wanted to touch his arms, brown with wiry muscles

underneath. I wanted to taste his full red lips. He was probably a hustler, I thought in a bright flash of clarity, or looking for a drunk trick to rob. But the eyes, those amazing eyes…it couldn't be. Even if he were, he was welcome to the twenty-odd dollars in my wallet. I wished in that instant I smoked, so I could offer him a cigarette to replace the one he just finished. How to ask him to come back to my apartment? How to initiate a seduction of this beautiful Latin apparition? My tongue seemed incapable of making a sound. "My name's Mark," I said, sticking out my hand.

"Angel." He shook my hand, and when our skin touched I felt an electric pulse course through my body, burning the effects of the alcohol out of my bloodstream, unfogging my brain, making my cock stir and start to come to life inside my pants. I wondered if he felt it too. He must have, there was no way it could have just happened to me. It couldn't have been that way. It just couldn't. He cast his eyes down again, then looked up at me through those dewy lashes that curled and framed his eyes. "You live nearby?" He had a slight accent.

"Uh-huh."

"Can we go there?" He reached out and touched my arm, sending chills down my spine. He smiled at me.

"Um, sure." I smiled hesitantly at him, wondering if this was the stupidest thing I'd ever done. I'd never picked someone up off the street before, and then I laughed at myself. Like you couldn't pick up someone dangerous in a bar? But there was something about this scenario, the possibility of danger, the chance this pretty boy might be dangerous, that seemed to make the entire thing even more intense, more erotic, hotter. My cock was growing to full size now inside my pants. "It's just up the street a little ways." I started walking.

He fell into step beside me, reaching out and taking my hand. His hand felt warm and soft, and I felt that electric charge yet again. Not quite as intensely, but I still felt it. The little hairs on the back of my neck stood up. My nipples hardened and became sensitive. The fabric of my T-shirt rubbing against them as I walked felt like feathers being brushed against them, making them harder and more erect.

I slipped my key into the door and opened it, reaching in to turn on the overhead light and the ceiling fan, then stood aside to let my Angel in. He smiled at me. "Beautiful place."

"Thanks." I felt the fear again in the pit of my stomach. Was I about to be robbed? Beaten? Murdered? But he was smaller than me, and when he turned those innocent eyes toward me again, I banished those thoughts once and for all. He stepped toward me almost shyly, hesitantly, and bit his lower lip. I leaned down and brought my lips against his. They were soft but firm, tender but strong. He tasted slightly of stale smoke and spearmint. He brought his arms up and around my back, pulling me closer. I slid my own arms around him and down his back. I put my hands on his ass. It was round and hard, solid. I longed to see it bare, unfettered from his clothes.

"You seem very sad," he whispered, his lips brushing against my neck.

I shook my head. "No, I am not sad now."

"It is still there." He tilted his head back, looking me right in the eyes. "In your eyes."

Again, I shook my head. What was there to tell? About the lover who'd left me a few months earlier, ripping my heart out? About the nights going to the bars hoping to meet someone, drinking myself into a stupor? The nights when I had hoped to find someone just like him, only to be disappointed? Instead, I kissed his neck, flicking my tongue out and licking his skin in a circular motion.

*"Madre de dios,"* he whispered. "That is so nice."

I slid my tongue down to where his neck met his shoulders.

I kissed him there in the hollow of his throat, squeezing his ass harder. His back arched.

He pulled his head back and smiled at me. "Do you want to fuck me, *papi*?"

"Very much," I replied, and kissed his lips again. I could smell his cologne—Calvin Klein Escape—and luxuriated in the velvety smoothness of his skin. He moaned a little as I continued kissing on his neck, squeezing his hard ass with both hands. His hands came up and pulled on my hard nipples. I slid my arms around him and lifted him up, his legs coming around my waist. I could feel his erection through his jeans, hard, insistent, urgent. He bit one of my nipples through my T-shirt, not hard, just enough to send another jolt of arousal through my body. We stood like that for an eternity, it seemed, him gently grazing my nipples with his teeth and lips, my cock becoming harder and harder. He slid down off me at last.

He grabbed my hard cock through my jeans, gripping it loosely. I let out my breath in an explosive blast.

I reached down and undid his belt, then his jeans. They fell down to his ankles. He stepped back from me and sat down on the couch. He took off his clunky boots, revealing white socks, and then stood up and stepped out of his pants. His legs were muscular, covered with wiry black hair. He reached down and pulled his tank top up and over his head in one motion. There was a trail of black hair from his navel down to the waistband of his boxer briefs. A few straggly hairs pointed out from his round nipples. There was another tattoo on his left chest; a halo. He smiled at me. I kicked off my shoes and then he was on his knees before me, slowly undoing my belt, my pants. He slid them down my legs, and I lifted one foot, then the other as he pulled them off me. He leaned forward and put his mouth on my cock through the cotton underwear.

I closed my eyes and tilted my head back.

"You like that?" he asked softly, barely audible over the sound of the air-conditioning blowing air through the vents.

"Yes, Angel, I like."

He slid his thumbs beneath the waistband of my underwear then jerked them down. My cock slapped against my lower belly once it was set free of the cotton restraint. I could feel my underwear sliding slowly down my legs as his tongue run along the underside of my cock. He licked it, always stopping just before his tongue reached the head of my cock, and then started back down the shaft. He took my balls into his mouth, gently applying pressure, just enough to make me moan but not enough to give pain. It felt incredible as my balls slid around inside his mouth, brushing up against his teeth, his tongue manipulating them from side to side. Then his mouth moved to my inner thighs, kissing, biting softly and gently, going from the top to just inside the knee and then back up and down the other leg. I was moaning. It had never felt like this before. No one had ever taken the time.

His tongue slid back up to the base of my cock and then back up to the head, and then he slipped it inside his mouth. He started sucking gently on the head, the whole time swirling his tongue around it, into the slit and then back to the outside again. Goose bumps rose on my skin. I was starting to tremble just a little bit. Then he took the whole thing into his mouth. I started moving my hips back and forth. I put my hands on his head. My cock slid slowly, gently, into and out of his mouth. He gagged once, and I felt his body react to the reflex, his stomach clenching, his shoulders coming forward. I slid back but he grabbed my ass and pulled it back forward, down into his throat, the whole time his tongue working and sliding around it.

"You wanna fuck me, *papi*?" he asked again, smiling up at me, stroking my wet cock with one hand.

"Yes." The word escaped my mouth, barely above a whisper.

He stood up and slid his boxer briefs down, stepping out of them. His own cock was swollen and hard. I reached for it, kneeling down to take it into my mouth. I licked the head and he moaned as I slid my tongue along the slit in the head, then slid it down the shaft until I reached his shaved balls. I reached up and took a nipple in each hand, pinching them gently, pulling on them. A gasp escaped his lips, and his body went rigid. He stepped back away from me, and turned, getting down onto the floor on all fours.

There were two matching tattoos on his back, on each shoulder blade, mirror images of each other. They were wings, outlined in blue ink but colored in with reds, greens, and yellows. They were the most breathtakingly beautiful tattoos I had ever seen, the work of a real master. I stood there staring at them as he arched his back, lifting his beautiful hard ass up into the air.

"Fuck me, please," he whispered. "Please."

I got down to my knees and pulled a condom out of my pants pocket, tearing the package open with my teeth. I slid it over my cock, feeling the latex gripping like a second layer of skin. I spat into my hand and ran the wetness over my cock, and took it into my hand and guided the head into his hole.

He gasped when he felt the pressure, his entire body going rigid for just an instant, and then he relaxed, and my cock slowly started to slide into him. Even as he relaxed and opened up for it, I could see the tense muscles in his back and shoulders. I reached down and began to knead his shoulder muscles, digging my fingers in ever so gently, moving them with slightly increased pressure. He moaned and gasped as I got deeper inside him.

I stopped when he cried out, my cock only about halfway

inside him. I moved my hips backward, slowly sliding out of him. His entire body was rigid. I stopped when only the head was inside him, and then began to slide it inside again. I began moving my hips in a circular motion, to try to loosen him up a bit. He moaned, his hands becoming fists.

"You like that, Angel?" I whispered.

"Oh, yes, *papi*, I like that." His voice came in a half whisper.

Once again, I was a little more than halfway inside him when it stopped, meeting an obstruction. I leaned down and began kissing the back of his neck.

"Oooooooh…"

I pulled back a little, then slid forward again.

A little further.

I pulled back again, and this time he opened completely for me. My cock slid all the way in, my balls slapping against him. I grabbed his shoulders and pulled him back, and he moaned. I sat there, fully inside him, holding him, until he began to move his ass back and forth. I released his shoulders and pulled back again, sliding almost completely out. He was gasping by now. I moved slowly, enjoying the feeling of him tightening and gripping my cock as it moved in and out of him, the pressure against my balls when I got all the way in. I closed my eyes briefly, opening them again to stare at the wings tattooed so vibrantly on his back. They almost seemed alive, moving with the rippling of the muscles of his back, as though they were trying to take on a life of their own, to unfold and spread, the brilliantly colored feathers shining in the light from the chandelier overhead.

His body began moving back toward mine as I slid into him, slowly at first, then faster, trying to drive me deeper inside him. I teased him with my cock, pulling it out, just leaving the head inside, sitting there like that for a few seconds until he started moving his ass back, trying to get me back inside. I moved my hips from side to side, around in a circle, and his moans grew louder and faster. Beads of sweat formed on his wings. Finally, I had enough of teasing his ass, and I started moving faster, matching the rhythm he was creating, driving deeper into him, trying to reach his core, the center of his very being. My cock seemed to grow harder and thicker and longer as I fucked him. The feathers of his tattoo seemed to glisten and glow from the sheen of sweat forming on his back. I was sweating myself, sweat forming at my hairline, my bangs growing damp, the hair under my arms becoming slick. Sweat rolled off my face, splashing onto his beautiful back.

This was how it was meant to be.

I could feel my balls working to start pumping out hot sticky fluid, but I wasn't ready. I wanted to keep fucking him, to keep pounding away on his beautiful ass, watching as the wings slowly took form, flexing and moving, propelling us up into the air until we were floating in the clouds, far above the twinkling lights of the French Quarter.

He grunted and gasped as his body shuddered as he came.

My entire body arched, went rigid, as the condom filled with my own come, spasming and convulsing as my cock emptied itself, my body shaking, the goose bumps coming out on my skin.

Afterward, we stayed together, my cock inside him, for a few moments, as we returned to earth and reality.

He slid away from my cock and faced me, his face and hair damp with sweat. He smiled, his liquid eyes looking up into mine.

I stood and took his hand, kissing it, and then led him back to the bedroom, leaving the puddle of his come on the hardwood floor. We didn't speak as I gently pushed him onto the bed and lay down beside him, curling my arms around him, pulling him to me. We kissed once, tenderly, without passion, a sweet kiss, like one shared by two teenagers who have just discovered the ecstasy their bodies are capable of experiencing.

It felt so right, holding him there in the bed.

"I love you, *papi*," he whispered, his lips brushing against my throat.

"I love you, my Angel," I whispered back, pulling him closer.

I woke to daylight streaming through my bedroom window, alone in my bed. I called for him, walking the length of my house, hoping he would still be there. But he wasn't anywhere. He was gone. He'd even cleaned up the puddle he'd left on the living room floor. It was as though he'd never been there at all. I sat down on my couch, naked, and hugged myself. I felt alone, more alone than I ever had in my life. Tears came to my eyes. "Damn you, Angel," I whispered. Somehow, I knew I would never see him again. It was too, too cruel.

There was a note on the coffee table.

*Papi, I cannot stay here with you, much as I would like to. It is forbidden. But thank you for giving me such joy. You won't always be sad. Angel.*

"Forbidden?" I said aloud.

And that's when I saw it, lying underneath the coffee table. I reached down and picked it up, held it up to the light, and smiled to myself. It was all I had left of him, my Angel, and I vowed to keep it forever.

A long green feather with hints of gold and red.

## DESIRE UNDER THE BLANKETS

Blair lit a cigarette. The light cast from his match flared briefly, casting shadows in the darkened room. He shook out the match and tossed it into an overflowing ashtray as he sucked in hungrily at the smoke. The menthol clotted in his lungs and he fought against the cough fighting its way up his windpipe, determined to expel the poisons. His eyes watered, and he gave in to the cough at last, muffling its sound. The clock on his desk read 4:15 a.m. The rest of the fraternity house was silent. The majority of his brothers were undoubtedly passed out from too much alcohol; some of them, he was sure, were huddled in rooms smoking pot out of bongs or snorting cocaine off the glass in picture frames. His own supply of cocaine was sitting in a small pile on a framed photograph of his mother on the desk top, next to a bong made of glass and plastic in the shape of a dragon.

He opened his small refrigerator and got a can of Pepsi. He was still a little drunk from the evening's festivities. Big Brother night, a tradition each semester, when the pledges received their protectors and advisors amongst the group of the already initiated, had ended around two in the morning when the keg ran dry and the last pledge had vomited. His own little brother, Mike Van Zale, was sleeping off his drunkenness in Blair's bed, snoring a little softly. Mike had puked around midnight, thanks to the Jose Cuervo shots Blair had poured down his throat. After Mike had staggered down the hallway to the bathroom and lost the contents of his stomach, Blair took pity on him and led him up to his room. Some of the other brothers would force their new charges to drink again after throwing up, but Blair was a little more compassionate. Besides, the previous semester one of the Alpha Chi Omega pledges almost died from alcohol abuse. Blair's brothers at Beta Kappa, for the most part, only paid lip service to the new university regulations regarding alcohol hazing of pledges. *They're idiots*, Blair reflected as he stubbed out his cigarette and made another line from the cocaine. It wasn't the first time he'd thought that nor, he reflected, was it likely to be the last.

His nostrils were already numb from previous snorts and he knew this one wouldn't restore the high the first one, hours earlier, had given him. All this would do was make his hands shake and his teeth grind. It was a waste but he was in the stage he called the "I wants," when he began to mentally crave more and more cocaine. He took a hit off the bong to lessen the edge of the coke when it hit. He held the smoke in as long as he could before it exploded out of him in a massive coughing fit. He grabbed a tissue and spat out a wad of phlegm.

On the bed, Mike shifted and moaned a little.

Blair took a sip of his Pepsi to cool his burning throat and walked over to the bed. Mike was sprawled on his back on top of the covers. In the moonlight coming through the slightly parted curtains, his skin looked like smooth alabaster. His hairless and hard chest gleamed in the ghostly light. Thick wiry hair sprouted from under his arms. A thin line of drool hung from the corner of his mouth. His face was expressionless. A thin trail of wiry black hairs ran from his navel to the waistband of his white briefs.

He was quite beautiful.

He was the first little brother Blair had taken whom he found attractive. Mike was his third in as many semesters since he'd become an active. Blair's homosexuality was something he kept hidden and guarded from his brothers. He knew some of the brothers that didn't like him speculated about him, and every once in a while one of them, when drunk or stoned or both, would make some snide comment to him at a party. He was careful to keep his sexual activity away from school. When he was home in Los Angeles he might hit a couple of the bars in West Hollywood for sexual release, but he kept that life carefully compartmentalized and away from the University of California at Polk. There was, he knew, a small gay bar in one of the seedier parts of town but he avoided it, just as he avoided the students who belonged to the Gay and Lesbian Student Union. Even though he was attracted to some of the other brothers, and had heard whispered rumors about homosexual activity in the house (usually occurring in the throes of liquor or drugs), he kept himself away from it all. No matter how drunk or stoned he was, no matter how attracted to one of the brothers, he stuck to his hands-off policy. Any pledge he thought the slightest bit attractive he refused to accept as his little brother, instead taking a scrawny, pimple-faced eighteen-year-old one semester, an overweight drunken mess the next. But Mike was different somehow, and even though he told himself it was a mistake, when Mike picked him he said yes.

Rush was alcohol free by university mandate these days. Strict regulations against smoking pot, usually ignored most of the semester, were vigorously enforced during rush. There were rumors of undercover cops pretending to be prospective pledges infiltrating the rush system to look for drugs, and Beta Kappa took these tales as holy scripture. It didn't stop Blair from going over to friends' apartments and getting stoned before the activities began. The only way he could cope at those events was to be stoned. He was cursed with an inexplicable shyness that years of drama courses and play performances had never cured. So, on the first night, Casino Night, with brothers and the little sisters acting as card dealers and roulette croupiers, he had wandered in about ten minutes after the prospective pledges started arriving and stood in the doorway to the big activity room. He made a name tag for himself and stuck it to his shirt and longed for a beer.

"Hi," a voice had said from behind him. "Are you one of the brothers?"

He'd turned and come face-to-face with what he later described in his diary as Apollo, God of Light and Beauty, in human form. Short-cropped dark hair, pale blue eyes, a smattering of freckles sprinkled across a snub nose, thick lips, and muscles bulging out of a tight polo shirt and loose-fitting blue jeans. He remembered to grin and went into what he called Joe Fraternity mode, even though he was utterly and completely in lust. "Yes, Blair Blanchard. And you are?"

"Mike Van Zale, I'm a sophomore from Visalia. Majoring in anatomy and physiology." He smiled, showing teeth that were white, some of them slightly crooked.

*Of course you are*, Blair thought. Mike was only about five-seven, the top of his head reaching about to Blair's mouth. "Let me show you around and introduce you to some of the brothers."

Mike had attached himself to Blair, going on the house tour, being introduced to the other brothers. His effect on the little sisters was almost painfully obvious, but Mike seemed unaware of the looks he was getting from the girls, remaining focused almost entirely on Blair and everything he said. He'd accepted a pledge bid that night, and on his daily visits to the house he always stopped by Blair's room first. As the weeks passed leading up to the selection of Big Brothers, Blair knew Mike was going to pick him. He also knew Mike had slept with some of the little sisters after parties, and the girls, who for whatever reason always seemed to confide in him, had told him Mike had "a big one."

And now there it was, covered only by a thin layer of white cotton, just inches from him.

*I want you*, Blair whispered. He was aware of his growing attachment to Mike, dreaming about him, fantasizing about him while he masturbated, picturing them lying in bed together naked, kissing, nibbling on Mike's big nipples, trailing his tongue down the flat stomach. He could feel Mike's big strong arms around him, pulling him in closer and holding him more tightly as their lips met, Mike's full sensual lips parting and his tongue sliding into Mike's mouth, feeling his slightly crooked front teeth with his tongue. Mike's beautiful slate blue eyes slightly closed in pleasure as he slowly began to grind his crotch against Blair's, their erections straining against each other longing for release.

Blair reached his trembling hand out toward Mike, pausing just above his half-dollar-sized right nipple. Mike's even breathing raised his chest almost to where it would touch Blair's hand and then dropped back down. *How does your skin feel*, Blair wondered, *is it cool and smooth and velvety, or would it be hot and fevered to the touch?*

As though in answer Mike moaned a little in his sleep.

Reflexively, Blair's hand shot back, and he reached for the bong again. He lit the bowl, inhaling gently until the water began to bubble, and the cool smoke snaked its way up the long glass neck of the dragon and entered his mouth and into his lungs. He put the bong back on the desk and held the breath as long as he could before expelling it toward the ceiling, a fog of curls.

Mike shifted again in his sleep, muttering incomprehensible sounds, the gibberish of the sleeping. His left hand slid up from the bedspread and rested on his lower abdomen, just above the elastic waistband of his underwear.

Blair looked at the hand as the smoke began to do its magic on his mind. Mike's hand was beautifully shaped, big and strong with black hairs curling along the side of it just below his pinkie. His fingers were strong rather than stubby and meaty, graceful, an artist's hand.

*Yeah, right, an artist's hand,* Blair's voice mocked inside his head. *He has the IQ of a doorknob. He doesn't get the jokes on* ALF *reruns, for God's sake. His favorite movie is* Transformers. *He has never read a book he didn't have to for class. He has the body of a god and the soul of a, well, face it, the soul of a peasant.*

*But not mean-spirited, no,* he amended. *Never mean-spirited. He's sweet and gentle and kind, with never a bad word for anyone or about anything.*

He was almost childlike in his simplicity.

Blair reached out again toward the nipple, the mound of muscle lying on the rib cage. He wanted to touch his nipple, tweak it softly, pull on it a little bit, just to see what would happen, to see if he would wake.

What if he did wake to Blair hovering over his near-naked body? To having his nipple toyed with?

His eyes could open slowly with a slow moan. "That feels good, Blair, I like that," and he would give him that lazy smile, the one that exposed the slightly crooked teeth, and take Blair by the hand and pull him onto the bed with him, using his free hand to release his huge cock from the white cotton restraints, and they would kiss as Blair fumbled out of his clothes until they were both naked on the coverlet, Mike rolling him over until Blair was on his back, his legs going up in the air as Mike spat on his hands and wet his cock, sliding it into Blair, who would open for its intrusion, its pleasure bringing hardness sliding deep inside him until he had to clench his teeth to keep from screaming, it felt so damned good, and Mike would gently rock his hips back and forth, teasing him, taunting him as he slowly slid out before plunging deeply back in, Blair's breath coming in gasps until he could hold himself back no longer and shot a long stringy rope of come out, raindrops of white falling on his chest and stomach as Mike smiled down at him before pulling out and finishing himself off as well.

And then Mike would move in with him, in this very room. They would put in another bed for appearance's sake, but every night they would slowly undress each other before climbing into bed, kissing and caressing and loving each other, before making love and going to sleep, and in the mornings they would wake in each other's arms, loving each other, happy and contented. They would both graduate from college and move down to LA, getting a great place in the Hollywood Hills, with a pool and a hot tub, and invitations to parties at the Blanchard-Van Zale's would be the most sought after, the most prestigious in the West Hollywood scene. Other men, models, actors, producers, agents, directors, would try to steal Mike away from him by offering to make him a star, by offering him cars and jewelry and money, and Mike would always just smile and say, "Thank you, but no, I am in love with Blair and can't live without him in my life." And they would grow old together, a permanent fixture in the West Hollywood social scene, Blair writing his books and Mike doing, well, whatever it was he wanted to do. And every night, they would share a glass of red wine before making love and going to sleep, celebrating their life together.

Their love.

Blair smiled. *It could happen that way*, he thought to himself as he lit another cigarette.

Or Mike could open his eyes. "What the hell are you doing?" he would say, shaking his head, trying to clear it from the raging hangover and the overwhelming sense that something was wrong, something was terribly, terribly wrong.

"I, uh, I…" Blair would panic, the cocaine and the pot and the alcohol rushing together in his clouded head as he tried to think of a plausible reason why he had been tugging on Mike's nipple, why he still was! He would pull his hand back as if burned.

Mike would sit up, awareness dawning on his face. "You're a FAG," he would say, his beautiful eyes narrowing in disgust and hatred, his lips curling back over the crooked teeth in a sneer. "A fucking faggot! Were you going to suck my dick next?" And then aware that he was only in his underwear, he would shove Blair back and away, Blair falling backward, hitting the wall with a thump loud enough to wake everyone else in the house as Mike grabbed for his pants and pulled them on, his voice rising as he continued to rant. "A fucking fag! Beta Kappa, some fucking fraternity! Are you all butt brothers? Is that what this place is? A fucking faggot recruitment center?"

Voices in the hall, pounding on the door. Mike pulls his sweater over his head.

"Mike, please—" Blair would beg from the floor, unable to move, unable to do anything as Mike opened the door and other fraternity brothers came into the room, and Mike was telling them, telling him what Blair had been doing, and his carefully protected life, the one of acceptance and fraternity and friendship that he had worked so long and so hard to build, would be gone as Mike screamed at them that Blair was a fag, Blair was a fag, Blair was a fag.

"He's lying..." Blair tried to say, but the words clogged in his throat, wouldn't come out, and then his brothers were turning to look at him, and his best friend, his closest friend, his pledge brother Chris Moore's face twisted with loathing and hatred and contempt as he spat the word out, "Fag."

He stubbed out the cigarette and stood up. He looked down at Mike and then peered through the curtains. The sun was coming up.

He reached out and shook Mike's shoulder. "Mike."

Mike's eyes opened and his mouth worked slowly. "Blair? What the—"

"I let you sleep in my room, but it's time for you to get back home." Blair smiled as he spoke the words slowly, softly, gently. "The worst thing in the world is for a pledge to be in the house the morning after Big Brother Night." He bent down and picked up Mike's clothes from the floor and handed them to him.

Mike stood up and rubbed his eyes. "I feel like shit."

"Go on home and get some sleep."

Mike yawned and stretched, muscles flexing and contracting all over his body. Blair turned his head.

He couldn't watch.

Mike pulled his clothes on in an agony of movement, tied his shoes and gave Blair a hug. "Thanks for watching out for me."

"What are big brothers for? Come on by tonight and I'll take you out for a nice dinner."

Mike smiled. "Thanks, Blair."

The door closed behind him. Blair lit another cigarette and walked over to the window. He stood there until Mike came out the door, and watched him walk away down the sidewalk. His right hand made a fist, and he gently pounded the window with it twice as he watched.

Then he put the cigarette out and undressed. He slid beneath the sheets. He could smell Mike's presence there, and the sheets were still warm from Mike's body.

"I love you," he whispered to the ceiling, then closed his eyes and went to sleep.

## DISASTER RELIEF

M ost of the damage is upstairs," I said as I unlocked the front door to my apartment and pushed the door open. I stood in the doorway and allowed him to pass. "Although we did get some mold down here on the walls." I shrugged. I'd shown the wreckage that had been my home for just two months to so many people by this time that it didn't affect me anymore. The first time I'd walked in after Katrina had gone through I had been in shock. You never expect to see your home in that condition; mold running down the walls, plaster wreckage covering the stairs, your bed a mildew factory. It had made me sick to my stomach.

Well, that and the smell coming from the refrigerator.

It was my home, it was the same apartment I'd been so excited to move into a million years ago in June, but I didn't feel the same way about it as I did before.

Christian Evans, my FEMA inspector, whistled as he walked in and took a look around. "Nice place."

"It was." I used to love the high ceilings, the two ceiling fans, the curved staircase leading up to the second floor, and the hardwood floor I polished until it shone like a mirror. Now the floor was covered with dust from the collapsed ceiling upstairs. The plaster on the walls in the living room was cracked, and the true enemy was evident on the ceiling—those horrible black spreading spots of mold that looked like ink blots. But at least the ever-present stench of mold and mildew was hardly noticeable anymore.

And I'd won my epic battle with the refrigerator.

"But I imagine you've seen a lot worse," I went on, hugging myself. It was a cool morning with a strong breeze blowing that made it seem colder, and of course I didn't have the heat turned on. Not much point in trying to warm the place when there was no ceiling upstairs. *Of course he's seen worse*, I scolded myself. That had been my litany ever since I'd come back.

*You're one of the lucky ones, remember that.*

Christian shrugged. He was a small man, maybe about five-eight, in his early thirties. He was cute in that nondescript metrosexual "is he gay or straight?" way. He had a light brown goatee and had gelled his brown hair into that just-got-out-of-bed look that seemed to be all the rage. Before the storm, I'd always referred to that style as the freshly fucked look. I'd never really cared for it much, but it worked on him. He had a way of grinning that somehow worked with the gelled hair. "I've been out to the Ninth Ward and Lakeview," he said as he pulled his laser pointer out of his pocket and started measuring the dimensions of the room. "So you lost your couch?"

"Mold. And the reclining chair, the coffee table." I sighed. I'd gone over the inventory of the losses so many times already I could say it all by rote. The new couch, gone. The comfy old reclining chair I'd inherited from my workout partner who'd inherited it from a good friend who'd died. I loved that chair, used to sit in it all the time, thinking and writing in my head. "I was lucky, though, I know." Even knowing it to be true didn't make saying it feel any less hollow. I hadn't lost everything, like so many people I knew. Houses destroyed, mementoes and everything inside gone forever. So many of my friends were now homeless, sleeping on couches belonging to friends or relatives, living in campers, waiting for FEMA trailers while they tried to figure out what they were going to do about what used to be their home. No, I had a place to live, and my source of income was still intact. I was able to come back to the city I loved, struggle to reestablish my life to some semblance of what it had been before. So many couldn't come back. So many others wouldn't. "But the kitchen is okay; I didn't lose anything in there except food."

He made some entries onto his laptop. "I'll put you down for everything in the living room. What about television, VCR, that kind of thing?"

"Those are all okay." I shook my head. "It was weird how some things survived and some things didn't. I mean, the towel I hung up after my shower that morning, which was wet, didn't get moldy at all. It was stiff, but all I had to do was wash it and it was fine." I cut myself off, recognizing the post-Katrina babble coming on. If I didn't stop myself, I was going to list every single item I owned and what happened to it. And he was only interested in what I lost.

But how do you explain to someone that you've lost your soul? The inner core of your being?

You can't.

He shrugged out of his brown sport coat. He was wearing a white dress shirt underneath, tucked into a tight pair of boot-cut jeans—and snakeskin cowboy boots. He placed the jacket on a wicker chair and I got a glimpse of his ass, which was round and hard. Definitely a nice ass. Before I would have stared at it, trying not to let drool dribble out of my mouth. I might have even tried to be flirtatious. He *might* be gay, after all. He turned back to me. "So let's see the upstairs."

I took a deep breath and started up the stairs. The upstairs still kind of bothered me, even though I'd seen it plenty of times. The ceiling was gone in the bedroom, hallway, and bathroom. After the turn in the stairs, the walls were gone, ripped out by the handyman hired to repair the place. It was still a shock to see the bare beams, the debris I hadn't cleaned off the stairs, and the moldy carpet in the hallway. "It looks a lot better," I said as I went around the turn. "I cleaned out a lot of the debris already." I had. The stairs had been buried in dust and plaster at least two inches deep—as had the hallway and the bedroom. But I hadn't gotten everything up, and I could feel bits of plaster crunching underneath my shoes. The bathroom ceiling was still there, if covered in mold. But the patio door off the bathroom had been blown off its hinges by the wind, and the linoleum on the floor was peeling up.

Yet somehow my towels—and my wet one, at that—hadn't gotten moldy.

Christian whistled as we walked into the bedroom and looked up at the bare beams. You could see clear up to the outer roof, which had just been finished a few days earlier. He pulled out his laser pointer and started measuring again, typing things into the laptop at a furious pace. "Bedroom set?"

"Gone."

"Any electronics?"

"Computer, scanner, printer, TV, DVD player."

He walked across to the bathroom and stuck his head in, then started typing again. "I'm putting you down for all toiletries, towels, all the bathroom stuff."

"Thanks." I started to correct him—the towels were okay—but stopped myself. Did it matter? I leaned against the wall and closed my eyes.

I could hear him typing away. Then he stopped. "Do you mind if I smoke?"

I opened my eyes. I laughed. "I think smoke is the least of

my concerns at this point. Besides, I smoke—*smoked*—in the house. Before."

"Oh, thanks, man." He shook a cigarette out of a crumpled pack of Pall Malls. "You laugh, but you'd be surprised. I was walking some woman through her house in Lakeview—total loss, it's going to have to be completely gutted and rebuilt— and she acted like I'd asked her to take poison or something when I asked if I could smoke, you know? I mean, what the hell difference did it make? The house was *ruined.* But she said no." He shrugged.

"That's crazy." I laughed. "Besides, I would think people would be nice to you." I went on, adding to myself, *since you control how much money they get to rebuild their lives.*

I was planning on being very nice.

"Tell that to them." He took a deep drag and looked around for an ashtray.

"Just use the floor."

He grimaced before sliding one of the windows open and flicking the ash outside. He gave me a little grin. "I just can't bring myself to do that."

"Habit, I guess—like the woman in Lakeview."

"Yeah." He leaned against the wall. "No, people aren't nice to us. They haven't forgotten the days after, you know, when we dropped the ball and the whole world was watching." He shook his head. "Of course, all of us didn't work for FEMA then, you know. We were hired as temps to help out with this mess...but they need someone to blame, I guess, and we're handy." He gave me a look. "I mean, you filed your claim two months ago and haven't seen a dime yet, right?" He shrugged. "That pisses people off—especially when other people have already gotten money. But the higher-ups keep changing everything from week to week."

"Yeah, well, being an asshole to you's not gonna make

anything different, you know?" I'd raged myself against FEMA any number of times in the days since the storm as I watched New Orleans die on television. "I appreciate you being so cool."

"Yeah." He opened his mouth to say something, but shut it.

"I'll just be glad when this is all over," I said, covering my face in my hands, "but I know it's never going to be, is it?"

"Hey." He stepped closer to me and took my hands away from my face. "It's going to be okay."

I looked at his face. *Damn, he's cute*, I thought to myself, and the look on his face, the mix of concern and sympathy, despite everything he'd already seen, touched me deep into my soul. Without stopping to think, I bent my head down and brushed my lips against his.

He stepped back. "Um—"

"Sorry." I shrugged, holding up both hands.

A small smile crept over his face. "I was just wondering if you had a condom?"

I paused for a minute, and a slow smile spread over my face. *In here*, I thought, *not in the carriage house. Oh no, here in the apartment, that would be perfect, just perfect, besides all I have at the carriage house is an air mattress on the floor anyway.* I gave a little laugh. "Wait here."

I ran down the stairs without waiting for a response, out the front door and over to the carriage house. I grabbed my backpack, shoving a handful of condoms, lube, and poppers into the front pouch, then slung it over my shoulder and went back out the door. As I walked back along the flagstones, I couldn't believe this was happening. *My FEMA inspector? Who would believe this?*

I wasn't sure I did myself.

When I got back up to my bedroom, he was leaning against

the wall, smoking a cigarette. He had unbuttoned his shirt, and it fell open to reveal a hairy but lean torso. Black hair curled around his hard pecs, down a trail to his navel, and then down into the just barely visible waistband of what appeared to be black Calvin Kleins. He gave me a hesitant little smile and ground the cigarette out under his boot. He stepped forward and shrugged the shirt down off his shoulders, revealing a smooth expanse of freckled muscle. He tilted his head down to the left, looking up at me with round brown eyes. He bit his lower lip.

I put down the backpack and pulled my sweatshirt over my head. I reached into the bag and pulled out the poppers and inhaled. I stepped toward him, handing him the bottle. He held it to his right nostril, the left, then put the top back on and set it down.

The rush hit me, and all I wanted right then, more than anything, more than my life back, more than my apartment the way it was, was to feel his bare skin against mine, to grind my swelling crotch against his. I stepped forward and put my arms around him, his skin soft yet firm to the touch, smooth and satiny, and I pressed my lips to the base of his throat, and I felt him start to growl as he thrust his pelvis forward against mine, and I began licking his throat.

"Oh my God," he whispered, his hands cupping my ass and squeezing, pulling me forward against him. "That feels so good, please don't stop, my God…"

As if I could.

He tasted slightly of sweat and maybe of soap. My tongue darted out, licking the top of his breastbone, then into the hollow just above the bone. He moaned, shifting his weight from side to side, our crotches pressed against each other. I could feel his erection against mine, and I moved my hips just a bit to create some friction. I brought my hands up to his nipples and started flicking them slightly, enough to make them harden beneath my fingertips.

He pushed my head away from his neck and took a deep breath. "My God, dude."

I gave him a lazy smile and undid his belt with one hand while pinching his left nipple. I pulled the zipper down, slid my hand underneath his balls, and squeezed gently. "You like that, boy?"

"Oh, yes, sir," he breathed.

I slid the pants down to his ankles. He was wearing black Calvin Klein boxer briefs that clung to his body. The head of his cock was poking out the top of the waistband. I licked my fingers and ran them over the tip. He shivered and twisted his head from side to side. I brought my lips to his throat again, and he gasped, a sound I took to be pleasure. I ran my tongue down his torso, from the neck to the pecs—stopping there to suck on each nipple for a moment—and then to just below his navel. I pulled the underwear down, freeing his thick dick before enveloping it with my lips, my tongue twirling around the underside of it.

I slid one hand between his legs and began stroking the lower crack of his ass. He shook and trembled again, giving me the incentive to slip a probing finger in between the hard glutes. I felt hair, and was glad he wasn't one of those boys who shaved their ass. There was just something *nasty* about a boy who didn't make himself antiseptic and hairless that made my dick's urgency to enter him even more frantic and necessary.

I leaned away from him and smiled. He gave me a weak, almost limp smile between gasps for breath. I grabbed hold of his hips and spun him around and looked at the muscular white ass. Sure enough, there were black hairs inside its crack, and I spread his ass cheeks with my hands and stuck my face in between, smelling him, darting my tongue out and licking at his hole. He arched his back, shoving his ass back into my face, and leaned forward, all of his weight resting on his forearms against the wall.

As I licked and probed his ass with my tongue, I felt my own need. It had been sublimated since the day I left, with the cat and everything I could think to grab in my car. I hadn't thought about sex, about getting laid, hell, even about masturbating in the weeks that followed, as I watched the city die on national television, as I worried about my home, and if I would ever be able to come back.

It felt somehow so right to eat his ass, as though somehow I was becoming myself again in a way I had forgotten.

I slid the condom over my cock and lubed it up, massaged lube into his hole, and slipped a finger inside. He let out another moan, and I smiled. He was ready, and so was I.

I slid the head of my cock into him, and his entire body stiffened. He rose up on his toes as a loud gasp was forced out of his throat, and a hand reflexively grabbed my left hip. "Easy," he whispered hoarsely. "It's big, oh God, it's big and I want it, but please go slow."

And even though I wanted to plunge it in, hard and brutal, ripping him apart and shoving him into the wall, I did as he asked and went slowly, bit by bit, waiting with each further insertion until he relaxed. I leaned forward as I slid inside, kissing the back of his neck as my hands gripped his hips. Finally, he let go with a sigh and I slid the rest of the way in.

I didn't move. I just stood there, my cock deep inside his body, and closed my eyes, tilting my head back.

*This is life, breathing again. This is connecting with another human being, and the warmth of his body feels so right, for the first time in weeks...*

And I started moving, sliding back and forth slowly,

listening to him moan, feeling him shivering and trembling with the pleasure my cock was giving him, and then his own need took control, and he began sliding himself back as I entered, until we were moving in a faster, more brutal rhythm.

His arms slapped against the wall.

"Yes," he repeated over and over again, breathing it out each time I pounded into him, louder and louder, his muscles flexing involuntarily, and I rode him, feeling my orgasm coming closer and closer, and I started pounding harder, pulling him back toward me and slamming forward so hard that he was rising up on his toes as I tried to shove my entire body inside him, I wanted to go deeper into him than any man ever had before, deeper than I'd ever gone before, wanting to reach the very core of his being, to touch his soul.

And then my mind exploded with the animalistic ecstasy of my orgasm, my entire body stiffening and my own breath exploding out of me, black spots dancing before my eyes because I couldn't catch my breath, and I had lifted him off the ground, impaling him, and he was shaking with me.

And my breathing slowed.

I set him back down.

I slid out of him.

"Jesus," he whispered, turning around, a string of come hanging from the head of his cock. He reached over and touched my face. "That was so intense...my God."

I smiled, unable to speak.

"Can I clean up at your place?" He gave me a weak smile. "I can't make my next appointment like this." He gestured at his sweat-soaked torso, and I noticed the come spots on the wall. He followed my gaze, and grinned sheepishly. "Um, I had already put down replacing the walls in here."

I touched his lips with the forefinger of my right hand. "Thank you, Christian."

He lowered his head. "Thank you."

We walked back to the carriage house. I gave him a towel and went downstairs, lighting a cigarette and sitting on the front stoop. I heard the shower water running.

I smiled.

*You're going to make it*, I said to myself, *you're going to be just fine.*

I felt normal again.

## PHENOM

The arms around me hit a grand slam tonight.
It didn't matter; we lost the game anyway. But I didn't care. I've never really cared much about baseball. In fact, I'd never been to a game until our local team signed Billy Chastain. As soon as I saw him being interviewed on the local news, I knew I was going to start going to games. It's not that I don't like baseball, I just never cared enough to go. But all it took was one look at Billy Chastain, and I was sold.

The interview had been one of those special pieces. He'd been a high school star, played in college a couple of years, and then one year in the minors, where he'd been a force to be reckoned with; with an amazing batting average and some outstanding play at third base, he'd been called up to the majors for this new season, and everyone was talking about him. I just stared at the television screen.

Sure, he was young, but he was also composed, well spoken, and seemed mature for his age. He was also drop-dead gorgeous. He had thick bluish-black hair, olive skin, and the most amazing green eyes. They showed clips of him fielding and batting—and then came the part that I wished I'd recorded: They showed him lifting weights. In the earlier shots, it was apparent he had a nice build; he seemed tall and lanky, almost a little raw-boned, but once they cut to the shots of him in the weight room, I was sold. His body was ripped as he moved from machine to machine in his white muscle shirt and long shorts, his dark hair damp with sweat. As his workout progressed and his muscles became more and more pumped, more and more defined, I could feel my cock starting to stir in my pants. And then they closed the segment with a shot of him pulling the tank top over his head and wiping his damp face with it. I gasped. His hairless torso slick with sweat, his abs perfect, his pecs round and beautiful, and the most amazing half-dollar-sized nipples, which I wanted to get my lips around.

I bought tickets and started going to every home game.

Our team sucked, to be frank, and it was soon apparent that there was no World Series or even division pennant in our future that year. But Billy was a great player and everyone was talking about him. He was leading the division in hits and had one of the highest batting averages in all of baseball. He made the cover of *Sports Illustrated* with the headline PHENOM, his beautiful face smiling out at people on newsstands all over the country. There were several shots of him inside without a shirt on, shots I had scanned into my computer, enlarged, and printed out for framing. I made sure my seats were always behind third base so I could get as great a view of him as humanly possible in his tight white pants that showed every curve and muscle of his legs—and the amazing round hard ass I thought about when I closed my eyes and masturbated. Every so often he would look up into the stands and smile, saluting us with a wave.

As much as I wanted to believe the smile and the wave were for me, I knew better.

Tonight's game was the last game of the regular season; our record ensured it was our last game of 2006. The Red Sox were on their way to the play-offs, and we had only taken two games off them all season. We were beaten 10–4. All four runs came from Billy's bat—a grand slam on his first pitch with the bases loaded. The stadium was half-empty; most of our fans had given up on the team at the midway point of the season. But not me—as long as there was a chance to see Billy swing his bat, I was there. And when he circled the bases, he paused briefly at third, looked up to the crowd, and waved at us.

I thought about waiting for the team after the game, seeing if I could get Billy to sign my program, but decided against it. I knew I was more than a little obsessed with him; my friends liked to call me his stalker. They were just giving me shit, but there was a fine line there I was afraid to cross, so instead I went to my car and drove to a small little gay bar close to the stadium. It was one of those places you went to meet friends for a beer or a drink, not one of the places where you went to do recreational drugs, dance to music played at ear-splitting levels with your shirt off and look for Mr. Right Now. The bar was pretty empty when I got there; it was usually only crowded during happy hour. The drinks were cheap but strong; a lot of guys met their friends there to get a nice cheap buzz going before they moved on to other bars in their eternal quest for tonight's orgasm. The bartender was a nice-looking man in his mid-forties who popped the top off a bottle of Bud Light when he saw me come in and placed it on a napkin at the bar. I grinned my thanks and took a long pull. The television hung from the ceiling behind the bar was playing a rerun of *Will & Grace* on Lifetime. There were only two other people in the bar, shooting pool in the back area.

I was on my second beer, watching as Grace decided for the thousandth time that her gay best friend was more important to her than any straight man could be—which always struck me as kind of tragic, sad and twisted rather than uplifting—when the door opened. I didn't turn and look to see who was coming in—I didn't care, and I wasn't looking to get laid. I was on my second and final beer before heading home, and I preferred to be lost in my thoughts about Billy and how he looked in those tight white pants rather than doing the *shall-we-go-to-my-place-and-fuck* tango with a stranger. It'd been a long day, and I was looking forward to sleeping in the next morning.

I took another swig and almost fell off my bar stool when the person who'd walked in stepped up to the bar a couple of stools down from me.

I'd recognize Billy Chastain anywhere.

He was wearing a sleeveless navy blue T-shirt with the words *Crew Cut Wrestling* written in yellow across the front, along with the image of two men in singlets wrestling. His jeans rode low on his hips, and as he leaned forward on the bar while showing his ID to the bartender, his shirt crept up in the back and the jeans rode down a little further, showing off the red waistband of his tight gray Calvin Klein underwear. The way he was standing showed off that oh-so-perfectly round ass to anyone who wanted to look at it. My mouth went dry and I took another swig of my beer as the bartender handed him a bottle of Bud Light. He stood back up and took a drink. He saw me out of the corner of his eye and turned to look at me, giving me a friendly nod as he put the bottle back down.

I turned my eyes back to the television screen as fast as I could. Another episode of *Will & Grace* was starting. My heart started pounding as he moved down the bar toward me. "I know it's bad form to say this," he said in the husky voice I'd heard on television a million times but always made the hair on my arms stand up, "but I really *hate* that show. In the real world, a gay man would have told Grace years earlier, 'You're single because you're a neurotic self-absorbed cunt who's completely unlovable with no redeeming qualities whatsoever. Why would any man want you?'"

I laughed. I'd thought the same thing any number of times. I turned and looked at him, managing to remain calm on the outside while on the inside I felt like I was going to turn into a pool of jelly at any second. "Will's no better than she is."

He nodded. "He's a lawyer in New York with a nice body, and a gorgeous apartment, and he's kind of handsome—and he'd rather hang out with that crazy bitch instead of getting laid, yet he can't figure out why he's single? How the hell did he get through law school if he's that stupid?"

I tapped my beer bottle against his. "Exactly."

He tilted his head to one side and squinted his eyes a little bit. "You know, you look familiar."

"Do I?" I struggled to keep my voice from squeaking. "Well, I know who you are. Billy Chastain, the phenom."

He laughed. "Yeah, that's me." He took another drink from the beer. "Man, this beer is good. I don't drink while I'm in training, but the season is now officially over, and man, does this taste great." He looked at me again. "I know who you are. You've been to almost all of our home games—you sit up behind third base, right?"

"Guilty as charged."

"Big baseball fan." He grinned, and I could feel my cock stir in my jeans.

"Not really." I grinned back at him. "More of a big Billy Chastain fan."

"Really?" He stepped closer to me and put his hand on the inside of my leg. I felt an electric shock that went straight to my balls, and my cock was now achingly hard. He licked his lips. "How big?" He moved his hand into my crotch and lifted his eyebrows, his eyes getting wider. "Nice."

*This can't be happening*, I thought. *This has to be one of the best wet dreams ever.*

"You got any beer back at your place?" He lightly brushed his shoulder against mine.

"Um, yeah."

He gave my cock a squeeze and I thought I might come right there in my pants. "Mind if we go back there?" He winked at me. "You got a car? I take cabs."

"Yeah."

"You up for it?"

I finished my beer in one gulp. "Sure."

All the way to my apartment, he played with my cock. It was hard for me to focus on driving. We made small talk, me barely able to get out more than two words at a time. I parked and we walked up the flight of stairs to my front door. My hands shook as I unlocked the front door. Once we were inside and the door closed behind us, he grabbed me and pulled me to him, our bodies pressed tightly together as he tilted his head down, pressing his mouth onto mine. I sucked on his tongue and his hands came down behind me and squeezed my ass. My cock was aching, and I put my hands on his chest. I pinched one of his nipples and he moaned. He tilted his head back as I kept pinching, not letting go of his erect nipple. "Man," he breathed, "that drives me crazy."

I slid my hands down and pulled his shirt up. He raised his arms, his lats spreading like wings as the shirt came up and over his head. He dropped his shirt to the floor, and I kissed him at the base of his throat, moving my mouth down to his left nipple. As I sucked on it, I pinched the other. He moaned and started thrusting his crotch forward. A little wet spot appeared on the front of his pants. I didn't let up, sucking and licking and sometimes playing with his nipple with my tongue. He leaned back against the door, his head back, his eyes half-closed. I traced my tongue to the center of his chest, and then slowly slid it down to his navel. I undid his pants and they dropped to his ankles, and I put my mouth on his hard cock through the underwear. I played with the head of his cock with my mouth until he put both hands under my arms and pulled me back up to my feet.

He smiled at me and then pulled my shirt up over my head, tweaking both of my nipples before putting his mouth on my right one. He toyed with it, played with it, and I couldn't believe how good it felt, and then he too was sliding his tongue down my torso, undoing my pants and pulling my underwear down. My cock sprang free. He looked up at me and smiled. "That's a beauty, man," he said before putting his mouth on it.

I moaned as he tongued the underside of my cock and licked my balls. I still couldn't believe it was happening. Billy Chastain was sucking my cock—no one was going to believe this.

He stood up and smiled, putting his arms around me and pulling me close to him. He kissed my ear and knelt down, picking me up. I wrapped my legs around his waist and kissed his neck. He stepped out of his pants and carried me through the living room and into the bedroom, the whole time sucking on my earlobe while I ground my cock against his rock-hard stomach. He gently set me down on the bed and took off my shoes, then pulled my pants and underwear off, dropping them to the floor. I sat up on my elbows, watching as he took off his shoes and socks, then the underwear came off. His cock was long, thick, and hard, and bent a little to the left. He had trimmed his pubic hair down, and his balls were shaved. He smiled at me, then climbed onto the bed next to me. I turned and we kissed again, his tongue coming into my mouth while I reached down and put my hand on his cock. He pulled me on top of him, our cocks grinding together as we kissed. His body felt amazing against mine, his skin soft yet hard at the same time, the power of his muscles radiating through his skin.

"I want you to fuck me," he breathed into my ear.

Oh, God.

I reached into my bedside table and pulled out a condom, opening the package with my teeth. I sat back on my knees while I slipped the condom on, then squirted some lube onto it. I then put some lube on my fingers, sliding them into the crack of his ass until I found what I was looking for, and started spreading the lube around. His eyes closed. "Just do it, man," he breathed, spreading his legs further and tilting his pelvis up.

I started slow, placing the tip of my cock against his hole, gently applying a little pressure until the head went in. He tensed for a second, then relaxed. I went in a bit more, slowly, working my way in as he relaxed and got used to me being inside him. When I finally pushed all the way in, he gasped, tensed, and relaxed; his eyes opened wide, he grinned at me. "Wow, that feels amazing."

I started moving, slowly, sliding in and back out, then back in. With each deep thrust, his beautiful body shivered and quivered, moans escaping from his lips as I worked his ass, reaching up every once in a while to tweak his nipples, which obviously drove him insane. As I felt my own orgasm rising within me, I pounded faster and deeper and harder, and finally as my come started to build, he shouted out "Fuck! *Fuck! Fuck!*" and his entire body shook as he started shooting his own load. The sight of him drenching his chest with his own come got me pushing harder and I screamed out as my entire body convulsed, my own load shooting into the condom.

I collapsed on top of him, my cock still inside him.

He kissed the top of my head. "That was amazing."

"Uh-huh."

We lay like that for a few minutes, my ear pressed against his rib cage, listening to his racing heartbeat and his breathing.

Finally I sat up and pulled off the condom, dropping into the trash. "Let me get you a towel. Or do you want to shower?"

"Can I shower in the morning?"

I smiled. "Oh, that can be arranged." I tossed him a towel and he wiped his chest down. He tossed it back to me and I wiped my crotch down before getting back into the bed. He put his arms around me.

"Thank you," he said, kissing me on the neck again and nuzzling against my throat. "That was amazing."

"Yes, you were," I replied.

He smiled and yawned. "Do you mind if we sleep a little? I'm kind of worn out—the game and all." He winked at me. "And all."

"Sure."

He turned onto his side and I curled into him, kissing him good night on the mouth. He placed his head down on the pillow as I turned off the lights. Within a few seconds he was breathing regularly.

I snuggled up against him and put my own head down on top of his arm. We fit together perfectly.

My friends weren't going to believe this—but then, I wasn't sure I did either.

I could lie like this forever.

It might just be a one-nighter, and that was fine with me. I wasn't going to get ahead of myself and make plans for our future together or anything.

But he wasn't leaving my place in the morning until I'd seen that big dick shoot another load all over that ripped torso.

And on that note, I finally fell asleep.

## Oh, What a Friend I Have in Jesus

I watched as the storm rolled in from the ocean into Acapulco Bay. The lightning flashes at the mouth of the horseshoe-shaped inlet lit up the night sky. In the distance, the black water below the jagged white strings turned green. I sat on the balcony of a beachfront high-rise, smoking a cigarette, unable to sleep. It was about four o'clock in the morning, and I knew I was going to have to let myself out relatively soon to catch a cab back to the SS *Adonis*, which was setting sail for Mazatlan at promptly eight in the morning. Part of me was tempted to just go on to the airport and catch the next flight back to Los Angeles. I wasn't enjoying the cruise, as I'd known I wouldn't. It seemed now, as it had in the days before departure, like an incredible waste of time.

Inside the apartment, beyond the open sliding glass doors, Jesus muttered something in his sleep and rolled over onto his back. I looked inside, noting the long, thick brown cock resting off to the side of the large balls. His flat, perfectly smooth stomach rose and fell with every breath. I felt my own cock stir again inside my underwear, but ignored it and turned back to look out to sea. There wasn't time for another round, and besides, he was asleep. When he woke, I would most likely be out to sea, on the cruise I regretted taking. *It's only five more days,* I reminded myself. *After Mazatlan, we turn back north and head straight back to L.A. You can get through it, surely.*

The cruise hadn't been my idea. Whenever I thought about going on a cruise, my mind automatically returned to movies like *The Poseidon Adventure* and *Titanic.* It had been Mark's idea, one of his harebrained schemes born out of his own boredom and need for change. Maybe that wasn't quite fair—Mark was just more adventurous than I was, always had been, and I was usually more than happy to go along for the ride. It was Mark who'd dragged me to Gay Days at Disney, Southern Decadence in New Orleans, and IML in Chicago. I'd never regretted letting Mark serve as my vacation planner, having a great time every time I went anywhere with him. It was hard not to have fun with Mark; Mark drew people to him everywhere he went with his infectious big smile, sexy blue eyes, and his ripped muscular body. Everyone always looked at Mark, everyone always wanted to meet him, everyone always wanted to fuck him. Maybe I was a little jealous of him, but he'd worked long and hard on his body, and the work showed. He was always prone to take his shirt off whenever he got the chance, displaying the huge mouthwatering pecs and gigantic biceps that everyone wanted to touch, to see flexed. But I'd known Mark before he'd dedicated himself to turning himself, as he said, "into the hottest man over forty in Southern California." When he suggested going on the *Adonis* cruise, I'd been more than happy to fork over the several thousand dollars, despite my aversion to being on the high seas.

Mark made everything more fun.

I flicked my cigarette over the edge of the balcony and watched the little glowing red ember tumble end over end down eleven stories before exploding into sparks on the marble walkway below. The wind was picking up as the storm crossed the bay toward land, and I shivered a little. I debated lighting another one; debated getting dressed and slipping out the elevator and heading back to the ship.

Instead, I went inside and got back into the bed, feeling Jesus's warmth as he breathed shallowly in his sleep. There was a bedside lamp on, and as I drew on his body heat to warm my chilled skin, I looked back at the semi-hard cock with a little drop of liquid in the slit. It was a beautiful cock, purplish brown and gigantic when flaccid. When erect, it was the stuff of pornographic dreams. I stared at it wonderingly. *That thing was inside me about an hour ago*, I thought, resisting the urge to shake my head. *It made me feel like no other cock ever had before. I came three times while he pounded into my ass—no one's ever done that before. I came the first time without even touching my own cock.*

Mark had been forced to cancel his cruise at the last minute—a medical emergency. He'd overdone it at the gym and created a rupture inside his own ball sack, and his doctor had insisted on operating on it right away. The surgery itself was minor and routine—an outpatient procedure I'd driven him to and home from—but the doctor forbade him to leave the country. And when I said I'd cancel, too—Mark wouldn't hear of it. "*No*, you go on without me," my best friend had insisted. "I'd never forgive myself if you didn't go because of me. You go on. You'll have a blast, you'll see."

It was impossible to argue with him. If I didn't go, he would feel bad, which then would make me feel bad, and so it was easier just to go ahead and pack and head down to the port and get settled in. Mark drove me to the pier, all the way insisting I would have a good time.

*But I'm not you*, I wanted to say. *I won't know anyone, and I'm too shy to just start talking to strangers. I'll be a wallflower and bored the whole time. I'm not beautiful the way you are, with the body of a god and a smile that is so bright it could*

*draw bugs in the dark to its radiance. Without you, I'll just be
bored to death and have a miserable time.*

But I didn't say any of that, instead talking about how
I was looking forward to seeing Cabo and Acapulco and
Mazatlan, gambling in the on-board casino and going to the
disco to dance the night away with my shirt off and my jeans
riding low on my hips. I pretended an excitement I didn't feel.
I smiled and laughed and joked, knowing that if I let him know
how much I didn't want to go, he'd feel bad—and even though
his surgery wasn't a serious one, I wanted him to focus on
getting better. So I got out of the car, checked in and checked
my bags, waved good-bye from the deck of the ship, waving as
the horns blew and the big ship pulled away from the dock.

And then I became invisible.

I had my meals. I tanned on the deck while reading books,
watching the other men laughing and having fun with their
friends. I went into the disco in the evenings and sipped at
margaritas while watching guys make new friends, hit on
each other, walk past me like I wasn't there. I walked around
aimlessly, watching the moon in the night sky and wishing
there was someone with me, all the time thinking how much
more fun it would be if Mark were only there. Within minutes
of walking into a bar together, Mark's smile and body and
charisma would have a crowd of people around us.

Without him I was nothing.

When we docked in Acapulco yesterday afternoon, I
went ashore along with everyone else—although everyone
else seemed to be a part of a crowd talking and laughing and
making plans for their day. Me, I just grabbed a cab with no
real idea of where to go, so I just instructed the driver to take
me somewhere *los Americanos* rarely went. He just nodded,
and after about twenty minutes he let me out in a business
area, full of restaurants and bars and shops. As I walked

around, I slowly began to realize that this was the part of Acapulco that the Mexican tourists came to—white faces were few and far between. I did some shopping, ate dinner at an Italian restaurant, and walked a little further up the street. It was geeting late, and I was just thinking about hailing a cab and heading back to the boat when I glanced up a side street and saw a place called Club Caliente.

"You speak English?" a young man beside me said.

I turned and looked at him. He was young, maybe seventeen or so, short and stocky with a face burned reddish brown by the sun. He was smiling. I smiled back. "Yes," I replied.

He nodded at Club Caliente. "Is club with dancers. For men. Upstairs, the women dance. Downstairs, the boys." His smile grew bigger. "You like the boys?"

I nodded.

"The boys dance. You will like."

"Thank you," I replied, and started watching the traffic for a cab. But as I saw one approaching and started to raise my hand to wave it down, I stopped. I looked back over my shoulder.

*Mark would go to the club. You owe it to Mark to go in there and check it out. If it's scary and dirty or whatever, you can always leave and walk back up here to get a cab. But you'll have a story to tell Mark, for sure—and wouldn't it be nice if one of the stories of this trip was actually true rather than made up?*

So, without really expecting too much, I walked down the side street, paid a five hundred peso cover charge, and walked into the bar.

It was dark, as all gay bars are; a few lights here and there breaking through the gloom. I could see that there were less than ten people inside. I walked up to the bar and ordered a bottle of Bud Light, and made my way to a table in the corner.

The music was playing rather loudly, and I was kind of amused to note that a gay bar is a gay bar, regardless of the country. I sat down on a stool and nursed my beer as someone leapt up onto the bar and started dancing. My jaw dropped.

He was stark naked except for his boots.

*So, a gay bar is not the same everywhere.* I smiled to myself. He was short and looked like he was in his late teens, with cinnamon skin and that smooth, lean youthful type of body that some boys are just blessed with. He danced his way around the top of the bar, his big dick flopping, kneeling down and letting some of the guys seated there play with it, and was rewarded with folded bills being stuffed into his socks. He made his way around the bar a few times before jumping down and heading for patrons seated at the tables. When he reached me, he stood in between my legs, reached down and rubbed his dick against the bare skin of my legs. He tilted his head down, then raised his eyes to mine shyly. "You like?" he said, slapping it against my leg again.

"Very nice," I replied, thinking, *He's thinking "American with money," isn't he?*

He moved away after another moment, and I watched as he plied his wares at another table. I shook my head, wondering how Mark would react to the boy. I picked up my beer, and out of the corner of my eye, I saw another dancer climbing up onto the bar. I had the bottle up to my mouth as I turned my head and just stopped short.

The dancer on the bar was without question one of the most beautiful men I'd ever seen—which is saying a lot.

He was much taller than the previous one; maybe about six-two with thick shoulder-length blue-black hair and big round brown eyes, and his skin was tanned a dark copper. His shoulders were broad and his torso layered with corded muscle. His waist was small and his hips narrow, with long muscular legs that looked solid as stone. His entire body was hairless except for the patch of hair at his crotch, and his cock—

Was fully erect, long and thick and one of the biggest I'd ever seen outside of a porn film.

He danced around on top of the bar, turning around now and then to show a round, muscular pair of buttocks.

I gaped at him, unable to take my eyes off him.

He was magnificent.

He hopped down from the bar and made his way around the tables. I watched him—he didn't linger for long at any of them, and I could hear my heart pounding in my ears as he approached my table.

He flashed a dazzling smile of even white teeth at me. "Hola! I am Jesus."

"Hi," I somehow managed to mumble.

He stepped in close between my legs, his big thick hard cock brushing against the bare skin of my upper legs. "This place is a dump, no?" His English was perfect, only lightly accented. I stared into his eyes. How old could he be, I wondered, resisting the urge to reach out and touch his lean torso, to reach down and put my hand on that gigantic cock. He tossed his hair back and placed his hands on my chest. They felt hot through the T-shirt fabric, as though they would burn right through it. "If I had better offer, I would get my clothes and leave right now." He flashed that smile at me again.

My heart sank. Stupidly, I had allowed myself to hope he might actually be interested in me. No, he was for hire, and he targeted me as what he hoped would turn out to be a rich American. "Oh," I said, looking away from his eyes. "I see."

He watched my face for a moment, then he opened his mouth and shouted with laughter. "You think I am a *puta*? What you call a whore?"

My cheeks flamed with embarrassment. "I—uh—"

He leaned into me and whispered into my ear. "I think you sexy. Very sexy. I watch you come in, and I decide, I want that one." He brushed his lips against my cheek. "I have apartment two blocks from here—is beautiful place. You come?"

"Um…"

"I get clothes."

He reached down and squeezed my cock through my shorts, smiled at me again, and turned and walked away. I watched him until he disappeared through a door off to one side of the bar—the same door another short dancer, who could have been a clone of the first one other than his hair was too short—and stared.

This couldn't be happening. This kind of thing happened to Mark, but not to me.

I had just finished my beer when Jesus came back out through the door wearing a pair of faded torn jeans and no shirt. He walked right over to me and smiled. "Come on—" He stopped and laughed again, a joyous sound. "I don't know name."

"Stacy," I replied.

"Come on, Stacy." He grabbed me by the hand and dragged me down the hallway and out the front door.

As we walked the two blocks or so, he talked—an incessant stream that I couldn't have interrupted had I wanted to. He wasn't wearing a belt, and the worn jeans kept sliding down his hips until he would notice and yank them back up. I kept glancing out of the side of my eyes as the jeans worked their way down his hips with each step he took, revealing the tantalizing crack, the beautiful curve of his cheeks. My cock was rock hard, and then he led me across the street to a stunningly beautiful high-rise that looked like it was made of solid marble. "You live here?" I asked.

He laughed again. "I am what you would call 'kept,' is

that the right word? My lover lives in the capital and only comes here every other week or so. I dance at Caliente when I get bored." He pushed open the huge glass doors, and the older man working at the front desk called out, "Hola, Jesus!" He waved and led me to the elevator, pushing me inside one and hitting the 8 button. Once the elevator doors shut, he shoved me back against the glass wall and put his lips on mine, his hands wandering down into the front of my shorts. He wrapped a hand around my cock and started teasing the head with his fingertips, just as he slid his tongue deep inside my mouth and pressed his entire body against mine.

I would have let him fuck me right there in the elevator if he'd wanted to.

But then the elevator stopped and the doors opened. He laughed again and grabbed my hand, pulling me down a hallway to a cast-iron gate. He paused and unlocked it, then stepped inside and unlocked the inside wooden door, then pulled me in as he turned on the lights.

The apartment was stunning. The furniture was all white, matching the white marble floors and walls. A ceiling fan turned over the couch, and on the walls were paintings, splashes of magnificent color that looked expensive.

He shut the door behind us and undid his pants. They dropped to his ankles and he stepped out of them. His cock was hard, a drop of wetness at the tip. He knelt down and untied his boots and tossed them aside as I pulled my shirt over my head. On his knees, he scooted across the floor and untied my shoes, and I lifted one foot then the other as he removed them. He reached up and undid my belt, then my fly, and then he was gently sliding them down and off.

He smiled up at me. "Is very nice," he said, and then took my hardness into his mouth.

His tongue felt like silk against my cock, and I closed my

eyes and moaned as he began to work his mouth over it, going gently and slowly as he worked his mouth back and forth on my cock. After a few moments, though, he stopped, kissing the head, and got to his feet. "Come," he said, taking me by the hand and leading me through a door into the bedroom. He switched on the overhead light and ceiling fan, and I was stunned. The curtains in the living room had been closed, but in the bedroom they were pulled back, and all of Acapulco Bay spread out before me.

"What a view," I gasped out as he went around me, and then moaned as he spread my cheeks and slipped his tongue into my asshole.

*Oh...my...God.*

My entire body went rigid as he went to work on my asshole. His tongue was ravenous, licking and probing, darting in and out, his lips working on the surrounding skin. I couldn't help myself, I bent over and leaned on the bed as my entire body shuddered with pleasure. I could barely keep my eyes open as the pleasure swept through my body in waves, and my balls began to ache with desire.

And then he stopped.

"You taste so good," he whispered into my ear from behind as a probing finger went into my asshole. "And your ass is so beautiful..."

He pushed me onto the bed, and I rolled over onto my back as he slipped a condom over that huge cock.

My eyes widened.

There was just no way that could fit inside me.

He squirted lube onto the condom, then onto his hand. He smiled down at me. "You will like," he insisted, and then he got on the bed, raised my legs, and pressed the huge head against my entry.

*Relax, relax, relax, don't fight it.*

Come began leaking from my own cock as he slowly and gently began to work himself into me.

I'd never felt anything like it before; he was filling me and stretching me… I took a deep breath and focused again on relaxing.

"Oh my God." I breathed the words out as he went deeper inside me. I bit my lip to keep from crying out, trying to stay relaxed, trying not to resist this massive invasion, bigger than anyone I'd ever had inside me before.

"Oh, you feel so good," he cooed, smiling at me as he began gently tugging on my nipples, as he kept moving deeper into me, slowly, ever so slowly.

And then, with a final thrust, he buried himself.

All of my breath rushed out of me in a moan, and I came.

*Oh…my…God.*

And then he started slowly pulling back, pulling himself out of me.

It was indescribable. I'd never felt so amazing, so good, so much pleasure…and when all that was left inside me was the head, he slammed back into me and I cried out as I came yet a second time…but I didn't want him to stop, I never wanted him to stop, I just wanted him to pound me, to keep pounding me with that godlike cock, to pound on me until every drop of come inside me was drained, till my balls were empty and I heard myself growl, "Fuck me…fuck me…fuck me…"

And as he slammed back into me, I rammed myself against him. I wanted him inside me as far as he could go. I wanted that cock to fill me, to fuck me.

He smiled and we developed a rhythm, pulling away from each other before slamming together again.

I started stroking my own cock, already sticky from the two times I'd already come, and kept murmuring, "Yeah, fuck me, man, keep fucking me…"

I'd never been this way before.

I'd never felt like this.

I didn't want him to ever stop. I wanted him to fuck me until I died, because there was no way I would ever feel like this again, I wanted to die and go to heaven with his huge monstrous cock inside me, pounding, pounding, pounding…

And just as I came a third time, he let out a cry and his entire body convulsed…and when he was finished, he pulled himself out of me, stripped the dripping condom off his cock, and smiled down at me.

"Oh, *papi*, what a wonderful ass," he breathed as he took a towel and wiped my come off me.

And then he lay down next to me, and within a matter of moments, was asleep.

And I had gone out to the balcony to smoke and watch the storm roll in.

I dressed quietly, retrieving my clothes from the floor in the living room where they'd been scattered. I walked back into the bedroom, knelt down, and brushed my lips against his cheek. "Thank you, Jesus," I whispered. He shifted in his sleep, but didn't wake up.

I walked back to the elevator and out to the street to flag down a cab. All the way back to the dock, I couldn't stop thinking about him.

He wanted *me*.

Maybe…maybe I wasn't such a loser after all.

And as I climbed the walkway back onto the boat, the storm broke around the boat, drenching me in warm rain. But I didn't care. It felt good.

I glanced at my watch as I got back to my room. Five in the

morning. I had just put the keycard into the slot when a door directly across the hall from mine opened and a guy wearing a pair of jogging shorts, socks, and shoes stepped out.

He had a magnificent body.

"Morning," I said, nodding. "Going out for a jog?"

One of his eyebrows went up and he smiled at me. "I want some exercise, at any rate."

I pushed my door open and stood aside. "Well, come on, then."

His hand brushed against my crotch as he went into my room.

I closed my eyes. *Thank you, Jesus*, I thought quickly as I shut the door behind me.

Maybe this cruise wasn't going to be so bad after all.

## SON OF A PREACHER MAN

The air was sticky, damp, and hot as I carefully slid the screen out of my window. The only sounds in the night was the electrical humming from the street light out in front of my house and the ever-present chirping of crickets. Before I climbed through the window, I stuck my head out to see if the light in my parents' window was still dark. They'd gone to bed about an hour before, but better safe than sorry. I'd been sneaking out all summer and they hadn't caught me once.

I jumped down into the damp grass and ran as quietly as I could down to the line of trees at the back of our property. I ducked into the trees and walked along the dry creek bed to the little dilapidated wood bridge behind the Burleson house, and sat down with my legs dangling over the side. It wasn't midnight yet, and Andy was always late. My parents were strict, but his made mine look like—well, I didn't know *what*, but something. His daddy was the preacher, and he thought his kids had to set an example for the rest of the Youth for Christ. Andy always had to help serve the Lord's Supper at least once a week, and instead of playing summer baseball like the rest of us, he spent his summer days working on his grandpa's farm out in the county. Preacher Burleson was a hard man whose eyes blazed with the power of the Lord and who didn't let his wife or daughters wear makeup or curl their hair.

Andy *hated* his daddy.

Nobody knew, except me. In front of everyone else, Andy was a good son, never contradicting his daddy, doing what he was told, minding. He studied and got good grades, knew his Bible inside and out, and had never been any trouble. But I was the only one who knew he cribbed cigarettes whenever he had the chance, could swear like a sailor, and hated every last adult in Corinth—probably in the whole state of Alabama, for that matter. All he ever talked about was running away, getting the hell out of Corinth, Alabama, the south. He never said where he wanted to go, but I was pretty sure anywhere else would do.

I sat there on the bridge, swatting at mosquitoes and listening to the sounds of the night. August in Alabama was like living in hell, I heard my mama say once, and she was right. The air was like a big hot wet towel pressing down on my moist skin. My armpits were already damp. I dangled my legs over the edge, swinging them like a little kid. My whole summer had revolved around sneaking out at night and meeting Andy. School was going to start in another month, football practice in two more weeks, and these nights were going to end. I didn't like to think about that. I wanted to believe the summer would go on forever, and every night I'd be sneaking out to meet Andy again—

"Hey."

I almost jumped out of my skin. "Kee-*rist,* Andy, you scared me."

He leaned up against the big pine tree while I stood up, wiping my sweaty palms against my cut-offs. He was grinning at me, his big white teeth shining in the moonlight. He wasn't wearing a shirt, and his torso was tanned dark, smooth and hairless except for a little bit of wiry black hair running from his belly button to the top of his cut-off jeans. His dirty-blondish-brown hair hung down in his face, and he pulled a crumpled pack of cigarettes from his pocket and shook one out. He offered me one, but I shook my head no. He might feel okay smoking so close to the house, but I didn't. He shook his head at me as he scraped a match alight. "Shee-it, Jamie, when you gonna stop being such a little pussy?"

"Fuck you."

He shrugged as he tossed the spent match into the creek bed. He squatted down on the edge of the bridge. "Whatcha wanna do tonight?"

He asked that every night we snuck out. Like we didn't always do the same thing every single time. "I don't know."

He punched me in the shoulder, not hard enough to hurt, but hard enough. "I know what I wanna do." He leaned in so close I could feel his breath against my ear, and it sent a little tingle down my spine. He grabbed my head and put his mouth on mine. He tasted like smoke and Dr Pepper. I closed my eyes and kissed him back, and felt his hands brush against my bare legs. I shivered a little bit.

I *knew* it was sin. I knew it when Andy and me had kissed that first night when he'd talked me into sneaking out of the house. It was wrong. Boys weren't supposed to do together what only married people were allowed to do. But it felt good. After that first time, when Andy and I had taken off all our clothes and done things, sinful things, I couldn't stop thinking about it. I prayed for God to take the thoughts away from me. I prayed for God to take Andy out of my head, to make me forget what it felt like to kiss him, what it felt like to have his bare skin against mine, what his dick tasted like, and how I forgot everything, God, my parents, sin, everything when we were doing what we did. I knew I shouldn't keep sneaking out and meeting him. I knew I was going to go to hell. I knew my dad would kill me if he found out, if Andy's daddy didn't beat him to it.

But every day I counted the hours until Mom and Dad went to sleep and I could slip off the screen and come meet Andy at the bridge.

He pulled his head back and gave me a lazy grin. "Are you scared?"

He asked me that every time. I shook my head. "I love you, Andy."

He stood up. "Come on. Let's go someplace."

"Where?" I asked as he started walking across the bridge. "What if someone sees us?"

"I don't care," he called back to me. "I don't care."

There was a field on the other side of the bridge, where Old Man Wheeler kept some cows. I followed him through the field keeping my eyes peeled for cow flop, and when we got to the other side I was all sweaty. He held the barbed wire apart for me, and then I did the same for him, and we were standing by the ditch along the old Tuscaloosa Road. "Where we going?"

He gave me a big grin. "You're still afraid of God, aren't you?"

"Yes."

"Come on, then." He grabbed me by the hand and we slunk along the ditch. No cars came along, which worried me enough so I didn't think about where we were going till we got to the parking lot. "No, Andy, no."

"Don't be so scared."

The brick front of the building rose up two stories at the other end of the parking lot, the huge steel cross on the front almost glowing in the moonlight. "Andy, this ain't right."

He started walking across the parking lot, and finally stopped. "Are you coming?"

I took a deep breath and started walking. I didn't think about the church. I didn't think about God or sin or anything. I just watched his back, the dark tan smoothly muscled skin disappearing into the white elastic of his underwear, just above the shorts. We got to the front door, and I said again, "Andy, we can't go in there."

He winked at me as he fished out a key. "Scaredy-cat."

He unlocked the door, and the cool air that came out made goose bumps come up on my skin. "We ain't gonna steal nothing. Come on."

He didn't turn on any lights, but we'd both spent enough time in the Corinth Church of Christ that we could walk around in the dark without a problem. He pulled open the double doors to the meeting room. The long rows of pews shone in the moonlight coming through the windows lining the walls just below the ceiling on either side. Up at the front was a raised space with the lectern where Brother Burleson preached. A huge cross was mounted on the wall right behind it so we could all reflect on the sacrifice Jesus made for us all, so we could get to heaven. The baptismal font was behind thick curtains to the left of the lectern, and the little number boards on either side still showed the hymn numbers of the songs we'd sung at last worship.

I took a deep breath. "Andy—"

Andy turned and grinned at me again. He undid his shorts and stepped out of them, his underwear glowing weirdly white against his tan. "Come on, Jamie, take off your shorts."

"Andy, we shouldn't be in here."

He walked over to me, standing right in front, and he pressed his mouth against mine, and put his arms around me, pulling me in close. He stuck his tongue into my mouth, and I melted against him, his hard chest pressing against mine, and I could feel his hard dick through the cotton of his underwear. He started kissing me on the neck, and I moaned, he knew I couldn't resist that, it was his favorite thing to do to me because he knew it made me crazy, made me forget everything else, made me want nothing more except to be with him…and then I felt him tugging on my shorts, slipping them down. I pulled back away. "Andy, this ain't right."

"You think you're gonna get struck by lightning?" he teased me. "If God hasn't struck us dead already, I think we're okay." He grabbed my hand and started pulling me toward the front. "Come on."

"Andy—"

He turned, his face angry. "Jesus *fucking* Christ, Jamie, haven't you figured it all out yet? You ain't that stupid!"

"Figured what out?"

He stuck his face right in mine. "God's just a boogeyman they made up to make us do what they want us to do."

*Blasphemy. In the house of the Lord!*

I trembled, and started praying to myself, but Andy was pulling me to the front. In the moonlight, I could see the hymnals and the Bibles in their slots on the backs of the pews. The cool air inside was making me shiver a little, and it felt like God himself was watching me. When we got to the step that led up to the lectern, he sat down on the edge and gave me that grin, the one that could always get me to do what he wanted me to. "You're still alive, ain't ya?" he teased me, reaching up and undoing my shorts and then sliding them down my legs. "Come on, buddy. You know you want to."

"It ain't right," I said as I stepped out of my shorts, and he stuck his face into the front of my underwear, rubbing his nose on my hard dick.

God help me, it felt good.

"Sit down here with me." He patted the indoor/outdoor carpet next to him. Trembling, I sat down and he put his hand on my inner thigh, kneading the muscle a bit. "Nothin's gonna happen. We ain't gonna turn into pillars of salt or anything. I promise."

*You can't promise that*, I thought as he put his hand behind my head and pulled my mouth to his. He didn't let go of my head, and I tried to breathe through my nose as his tongue slid into my mouth and I licked it with my own. He moaned from deep down inside, and his free hand grabbed hold of my biceps and squeezed it. We kept kissing, there in the shadow of the cross, and I closed my eyes, thinking *let God strike me down now, go ahead, I don't care, I love him and if that's sin, then I am a sinner and You can send me to hell.*

Andy pulled me back with him until we were lying on our sides facing each other, our mouths still locked together, and our arms went around each other. His smooth back felt like silk to my hands, and I slid them up and down his back as we kept kissing. My dick was straining, and I could feel his rubbing up against mine. I wanted to hold him, make him a part of me, somehow pull his body so close that we became one person, because that was what I always felt like, that somehow we were two halves of a whole—incomplete without the other. Just being around him made me happier than anything else—happier than catching the game-winning out, happier than catching a touchdown pass, happier than those times when I felt the Lord's spirit move me in church. I wanted to lie with him like that forever, in our own little time-space, where no one else existed and nothing else mattered.

Andy's hand went into the front of my underwear and I gasped when he grabbed hold of my dick. He ran his thumb over the tip of it and moved his mouth down onto my neck, nuzzling on it, and my entire body went stiff. "Oh…oh… oh…"

He slid the underwear down and started moving his hand up and down on my dick, pressing hard against my balls on the downward move, doing that thing with his thumb on the top on the way up. His tongue started making little circles on my neck, and he rolled me over onto my back so that he was on top of me, holding me down. He was always stronger than I was, even though I played sports and lifted weights. He locked his legs around mine and with his other arm held me down so I couldn't move, and he was rubbing his dick against my leg, little up-and-down movements, and I reached down and touched his butt, glowing white in the moonlight as it flexed and relaxed with every movement he made.

My breath started coming faster, and I could hear my heartbeat pounding in my ears, and I could feel his, pounding so hard against his skin it felt like it might just jump out of his chest. He was breathing faster too, and I opened my eyes and stared up at the cross as I felt it start, I knew it was going to happen even though I didn't want it to, even though I wanted this moment to last forever, the two of us lying there under the cross, in God's house, and it seemed as though it was right. God was about love, and understanding, no matter what Brother Burleson might thunder the next morning from his pulpit, screaming about the wages of sin and how we were all unworthy of His love, but at that moment I felt closer to God than I ever did when I was in the church, as though this were holy, and God knew, and God loved us anyway.

And I felt Andy's whole body go rigid as his stuff came out on my leg, and then I wasn't thinking about anything anymore except the way it felt as mine started coming up my dick, and my whole body went stiff and I couldn't help myself, it felt so good, so right that I had to cry out, nothing had felt this way before, it had always felt amazing but this was the best so far, and then it was coming out, drops falling on my stomach and chest, and my body was convulsing.

And it was over, and we lay there, under the cross, panting, holding on to each other.

"I love you, Jamie."

"I love you, Andy."

We cleaned ourselves up as best as we could, using our underwear, and put our shorts back on and walked back out of the church. Andy locked the door behind us, and he offered me a cigarette, which I took. We sat on the curb and smoked in silence.

"Wouldn't it be nice," he said finally, "if we could go somewhere we could always be together like this?"

I stared at him. "Andy, where?"

"There's got to be someplace," he said, scratching his head. "Jamie, we can't be the only ones, you know? Somewhere there are other boys like us." He stubbed his cigarette out. "After high school, I'm going to go find them."

I felt a stab of fear. Andy always talked about going away, and it always scared me. I didn't want him to go away. "Andy—"

He turned and grinned at me. "Calm down, Jamie. We've got our senior year to get through first." He leaned over and kissed my cheek. "Besides, I ain't going nowhere without you, partner." He stood up and offered me a hand to pull me up. "We better get going on home."

We walked home in silence, and I waved good-bye to him as he climbed through his own bedroom window. I walked back to my house, listening to the crickets and a dog barking somewhere off in the night. The house was still dark, which was good, and after I climbed through my own window, I leaned back out and looked up at the stars.

*Is it wrong, God?* I asked, wiping tears out of my eyes. *Can love be wrong?*

Like always, He didn't answer.

With a sigh, I got into my bed and closed my eyes.

# THE POOL BOY

I waited until I heard Jason's car back out of the driveway before I got out of bed. I was being a coward, I knew, but I still wasn't ready to face him with what I knew. I didn't want to have that argument, that confrontation. I wasn't sure I was ready yet to talk calmly and rationally. It still hurt too much. I wasn't sure I could discuss this with him without getting angry, without saying something that shouldn't be said, words in anger that couldn't be taken back. I wasn't sure I was quite ready yet to turn my back on ten years of loving and laughing and fighting, of good times and bad, of sleeping in the same bed with him and drawing comfort from the warmth of his body.

I called in sick to work. I might not have been physically ill, but I was certainly an emotional basket case. There wasn't any way that I could help my clients in this state. Their needs and concerns and problems all seemed so unimportant, so completely pointless to me that going into the office was probably a bad idea. I brushed my teeth and took a shower, put on my robe, and went downstairs for a fresh pot of coffee. While I waited for it to brew I got the notice out of the bill drawer, the notice that proclaimed his guilt to the world, the indisputable proof of his guilt; that he'd betrayed me, lied to me, ignored how I felt and did what he wanted to anyway.

Funny that a twenty-dollar parking ticket could mean so much more than what it was on the surface.

I stared at it. Yes, that was Brent's address on the ticket. The time of the offense was four thirty in the morning. The date was that weekend I'd gone home to my nephew's wedding. Jason had been illegally parked in front of Brent's house at four thirty in the morning while I was out of town. There was absolutely no logical explanation for Jason's car to be there at that hour.

He was still fucking Brent. Even though we'd talked about it. Even though he'd promised me he would end it. Even though he assured me he still loved me and he didn't love Brent.

This just happened to be the one time he was caught.

How many other times had he gone over there without me knowing, fucking Brent's pretty little ass?

How many other lies had he told?

I lit a cigarette and poured a cup of coffee. I sat down at the kitchen table and opened the blinds to the patio doors. The sun was shining down on the pool water, which sparkled blue. The backyard was beautiful. How many weekends had we spent out there, planting roses and flowers and bushes, digging out weeds, laying down marble? How many pool parties for friends had we thrown out there?

Jason had met Brent at one of those damned parties two years ago. I was playing hostess, blending daiquiris in the blender, filling glasses while Jason stoked the coals in the barbecue. Danny Martin, a pretty blond in his late thirties, had showed up with a pretty guy in his mid-twenties in tow. Danny was always falling in love; it seemed every two weeks or so he'd found the "one." He introduced me to the new "one," Brent. Brent was pretty. He had smooth skin without blemishes, brown hair parted in the middle in what we used to call a Buster Brown cut when I was a child, big green eyes, and an almost completely hairless body in his white Speedo. The white Lycra made his tan look darker, and his teeth were unbelievably white when he smiled and shook my hand. I couldn't help myself; I watched his round hard butt when he walked away. I found myself watching him all afternoon, splashing in the pool, diving off the board without leaving a splash, climbing out with water dripping seductively off his body.

If I'd known then what I knew now, I'd have thrown them both out.

"Thanks, Danny." I toasted him with my coffee cup.

*What is this hold Brent has over Jason*, I wondered for the thousandth time as I refilled my coffee cup. Was he such an incredible fuck? Could he suck the chrome off a Chrysler? Why was Brent so determined to hold on to Jason? Did he love him? Did he love him enough to wait for him all these years, even though it seemed unlikely Jason would ever leave me? And even if he did leave, if our relationship did end, there was so much more to it than Jason moving out—because I was damned if that little slut was going to live in this house. The house was in both our names. Our checking and savings accounts had both our names on them, and had for years. After ten years, who knew who owned what anymore? It would be a long, possibly ugly process to set us free from each other.

Jason swore he didn't love Brent, time and again, but he kept going back to him, even though he knew it hurt me, even though he knew I didn't want him to. He couldn't explain it to me, he couldn't articulate or find the words to explain why he kept going back to Brent. I wondered why Brent bothered. He was still young. He was still pretty. Why was he hanging on, why was he so happy to settle for just being the mistress? Surely, he could do better.

What was Jason telling him?

I didn't want to know.

I walked out into the hallway. There was a floor-length mirror in the foyer. I dropped my robe and stood there naked, looking at myself. My body was still firm. I'd gotten a little pudgy around the middle maybe, but I still could fit into 31 waist pants without having to hold my breath, without rolls of fat folding over the waistband. There were gray hairs sprouting in my hair. There were lines around my eyes and mouth, dark circles under my eyes that seemed to get darker every year. I flexed my arms and my legs. I was still in good shape. I still looked good. On those rare occasions when Jason and I would go out to bars, someone attractive always made eye contact with me and would smile. Waiters in restaurants flirted with me. I got cruised in the grocery store, at the beach.

I sighed and walked back into the kitchen, dragging the robe with me.

I heard a car pull up in the driveway.

*Did Jason forget something?* I panicked. I walked into the living room and peered out through the curtains, and let out a sigh of relief. It was a white truck with *Bayside Pool Service* printed on the side. There were nets and buckets of chemicals in the back. It was just Harry, the pool guy. I liked Harry. He was in his early fifties, with a beer gut and a balding head, three kids in college, and a pretty good sense of humor. I'd run into him and his wife, a chubby woman with a big smile and tobacco-yellowed teeth, in the grocery store a couple of times. They obviously loved each other very much, even after thirty years or so together. I wondered if Harry had ever cheated on Rosie.

I doubted it.

I sat back down at the kitchen table. My stomach growled. All that coffee on an empty stomach was not good. I poured myself a bowl of Cheerios, added milk, and walked back to the table. I sat down and started shoveling cereal into my mouth. When Harry got around to the pool, I'd go out and chat with him, offer him something to drink. Maybe just being around Harry would make me feel better about Jason.

I heard the gate open and made a mental note to squirt some WD-40 on the hinges. I sat there, eating my cereal, waiting for Harry's unmistakable shape to come into view.

Only it wasn't Harry.

It was a kid. He couldn't be much older than twenty—he still had that fresh scrubbed look of innocence in his face. He was maybe six feet tall. He was wearing a faded pair of 501s, a white ribbed tank top, and white running shoes. His hair was a dirty blond, and his arms were muscular and defined. Golden hairs glistened on his arms in the sunlight. A bead of sweat was running down the side of his tanned face. His eyes were pale blue, like a Siberian husky's. His face was chiseled, with a strong chin and slightly prominent nose. He set down the bucket of chemicals and started fishing leaves out of the pool with a net.

I sat there, watching him, as though turned to stone.

He walked around to the side of the pool closest to the doors and turned his back to me as he fished for leaves. His jeans had worn through on the left side, at the bottom of his round hard ass. He wasn't wearing underwear, and I could see the smooth, shockingly white skin of his cheek through the vertical cut in the fabric. I slowly got to my feet, pulling my robe closed. I was getting hard. Just as I stood up, he straightened up and dropped the net. In one fluid motion, he stripped the tank top off over his head, wiping his face with it. His back and shoulders were tanned and broad, tapering down into a V that slipped inside the jeans. The skin on his back was completely hairless. He finished wiping his face and tucked the shirt into the back of his pants. For just a single moment I saw the white skin underneath his jeans, the tantalizing start of the crack of his ass, and then the shirt was tucked in and hid everything.

I walked in slow motion to the door, unlocked it, and slid it open. He turned and smiled at me. His smile was amazing. It was like he had turned on klieg lights inside his eyes. "Good morning, sir."

I smiled back at him. "Where's Harry?"

"Vacation for a couple weeks. I'm filling in for him." He wiped his wet hand on his pants and stuck it out. "My name's Phil."

I shook his hand. His grip was firm and strong, his hand calloused and a little rough. "Nice to meet ya, Phil. I'm Ken."

"Likewise." He looked up at the sky. "Gonna be a scorcher today, I reckon."

"Yeah."

"Your yard's beautiful, Ken." He pulled the tank top out of his pants and wiped sweat off his face.

"Thanks." I tried to keep my eyes on his face, away from the round, hard pectoral muscles with the quarter-sized pink nipples, the flat defined stomach with the golden hairs leading down into his jeans.

"Most people think all they need is for us to come out once a week or so, and that'll keep the pool." He shrugged. "But you take good care of yours. Hardly nothing to do here."

"You could do me," I almost said, but didn't. "Would you like something to drink? I have iced tea, juice, or soda."

"Iced tea would be great." That smile again.

I smiled. "Be right back." I walked into the house and poured him a glass of tea.

He followed me and stood at the door, not coming in. I hoped my hard-on wasn't too obvious as I handed him the glass. He tilted his head back and swallowed it in one gulp. He smiled, handed me the glass back, and went back to work.

I followed him outside, sitting in the shade. He tested the pool's chlorine content and dumped the water out with a smile. "See? Nothing much to do for you today."

He picked up the net and the bucket of chemicals and started to move toward the gate.

"Busy day?" I blurted out.

He grinned at me. "Just three more pools today. This is a short route."

"Maybe you'd—" I hesitated before going on, "like to go for a swim, then? Get yourself cooled off?"

His grin faded. "Well, that would be nice...I don't have to get the truck back to the shop until four, and there's plenty of time for me to do the other pools, but I don't have a suit or nothing."

I started to say I would loan him a suit, I have about ten in different cuts and colors, but before I could he went on, "Course I don't need one, if you don't mind." His gaze locked on mine, as though daring me to say I'd mind.

"I don't mind."

He grinned at me again, putting everything down and sitting down. He yanked off his shoes and socks and stood back up. He looked at me for a moment before undoing his pants, sliding them slowly down his muscled legs. His cock was long and thick and semi-aroused, and the whiteness of his untanned skin stood out in marked contrast to the deep tan around it. His cock and heavy balls were pink, and his pubic hair was golden. He stood there for a moment while I stared at him, and with a shout he dove headfirst into the pool. He swam the entire length underwater, surfacing at the other end. "Water's perfect," he called to me. "Why don't you join me?"

*Why not?* I thought about Jason for a moment, and Brent. I dropped my robe and dove into the water, my erection be damned.

The water was perfect. Not too warm, not too cool. I opened my eyes and could see his legs at the other end. I swam toward them, watching them grow bigger as I approached. When I surfaced, he grinned at me. "Told ya."

I grinned back at him. "Yeah, you're right."

He hoisted himself up out of the water, shaking his hair.

I'd hoped that the coolness of the water would shrink my erection, but it hadn't. I stood there, looking at the water sparkling on his almost perfect form in the sun.

He looked back at me.

I stared into his blue eyes.

He slid back into the water and walked over to me. He reached down into the water and put his hand on my cock. "Nice." He smiled at me. He pulled me toward him, and then slid his arms around me, tilting his head down to mine.

Our lips met.

His mouth was hungry, urgent as it enveloped mine, his hands sliding up and down my back. I tilted my head backward, probing inside his mouth with my tongue. In answer, his tongue slid into my mouth and I closed my lips around it, sucking on it, refusing to let it go. He began to moan low in his throat. I brought one of my hands up to his right nipple, pinching it, feeling his cock growing harder and longer against my torso as he pulled me in tighter. My own cock pressed against the firm muscles of his inner thigh. His skin was smooth, firm yet soft to the touch, almost like silk. I moved my mouth down from his, running my tongue down his throat. His eyes closed, his head tilted back, drops of water falling from his chin. I slid my tongue down along the line of his shoulder to where the arm joined it, then down the crease between the muscles of the chest. He moved his arm out and my tongue went into the pit of his arm, which smelled slightly of sweat and chlorine. The wet blond hairs tasted salty as I licked them, pushing my tongue through to the skin. He moaned again. "Oh, that feels so good, damn."

I moved my mouth along the line of his chest to the right nipple, which was hard from the pinching. I licked it, running my tongue around the line where his skin turned pink, the base of his nipple. He moaned again, and then I covered my teeth with my lips and nipped the tip, pulling it out slightly. Goose bumps appeared on his arms despite the heat from the sun. I licked my way over to his other nipple, mimicking what I had done to the other. His hips began to move backward and forward, as though he were programmed to make a fucking motion when aroused. I slid my tongue down the cleavage in the center of his chest down to the deep valley between his abdominal muscles. His breaths were coming harder and faster. I looked up at his face. His eyes were still closed.

"Sit on the side of the pool," I commanded, and he obliged, putting his hands on the side and boosting himself out of the water, his legs spread slightly. His cock was standing straight up. I pushed his legs apart and slid between them, lowering my head. My tongue darted out and licked the head of his cock, short, quick, abrupt movements as though I were attacking an ice cream cone. He stiffened at first for a moment, and then relaxed. I started sliding my tongue around the head, which seemed to grow even thicker as I worked on it.

I took it into my mouth, my tongue still swirling, and he emitted a gasp, followed by a quick intake of breath. I slid my mouth down and gagged. I took in some more air in through my nose and took more of it into my mouth, swallowing it. I wanted all of it in my mouth. I wanted to give him the best blow job he had ever experienced. I wanted to give him the best head he would ever experience. I began moving up and down on it, my chin brushing against his thick balls when I got to the bottom, giving him the tongue action when I got to the top. He grabbed the top of my head and applied pressure, pushing my mouth down again and again. I could tell that he was ready to come, and when the spasms started I pulled back, getting shot in the face as he groaned and gasped, his stomach muscles contracting as he showered his load into my face and hair and onto my chest.

He looked at me, a half smile on his face. "Wow."

I smiled back at him. He was still hard.

Ah, youth.

"I want you to fuck me," I said.

"I've never done that." His face blushed.

"Have you ever been with a man before?" I asked, smiling to myself. The idea of corrupting this young man was oddly appealing.

He shrugged. "Guys have blown me." He looked away. "I—I don't know if I can do that, man."

I remembered my first time for a moment. I was about his age. I'd been nervous, frightened. "C'mon." I pulled myself up out of the pool. I took his hand and walked with him around to where my terry cloth robe was lying. I picked it up and toweled him dry. His dick stayed hard the entire time. I wiped his come off me and dried myself enough to not track water into the house. He followed me in through the patio doors, down the hall into the bedroom. I grabbed a couple of towels out of the bathroom and finished drying us both off. I opened my nightstand drawer, extracting the poppers, lube, and some condoms. He just stood there staring.

"I want you to fuck me," I said again.

He looked stricken. I knew what he was thinking. Getting blow jobs from guys from time to time didn't make him queer.

That was okay, almost normal even—what man would turn down a blow job? But to actually stick his cock up my ass, to fuck me like he would a woman, to ride me until we both came, that was a different story. That would make him a full-blown, Whitney Houston lip-syncing, rainbow-flag-carrying, Speedo-wearing faggot. "Well?"

He licked his lips. "Um, okay." He swallowed. "You have to promise you won't tell anyone!"

Ah, the innocence of youth, the terror of being exposed. "I promise."

I walked over to him, tearing open a condom packet with my teeth. I squirted a drop of lube into it, then slid it over his hard-on. I squirted some lube into my hand and stroked it over his cock. He smiled shyly at me. I rubbed lube into my hole.

I took his hand and led him over to the bed. I lay down on my back and spread my legs. He climbed onto the bed and sat there on his knees for a moment.

"Come on," I coaxed.

He closed his eyes, took a deep breath, and lifted my legs up, pressing his dick in the general direction of my hole, and began pushing. I slid my hand down and pointed it in the right direction. "Go slowly," I said, taking the cap off the poppers, and held it to my nose, inhaling first up one nostril, then the other.

"What's that?" he asked.

"It makes it better," I said, handing him the bottle as the wave of pleasure washed over my body. I wanted him in me as soon as possible. He imitated me and then handed the bottle back.

"Wow." He shook his head.

"Fuck me," I said with more urgency. I could feel the head of his cock against my hole, and I wanted that big thick shaft inside me.

"Wow," he said, his nipples growing erect again, and then he shoved his cock into me.

I bit my lip. It fucking hurt. I focused on relaxing. No one had fucked me besides Jason in years. I uncapped the poppers and took another hit up each nostril. He was still pushing, trying to get deeper inside me, but it still hurt oh how it hurt my eyes were watering I was going to have to push him off me—

And then I relaxed.

"Oh oh oh." I gasped out as the first wave of pleasure rolled over me. He was so fucking big, my God, it felt as though he were filling me completely, and still, he kept pushing deeper into me, until finally he was all the way in, flexing his ass cheeks, trying to get deeper.

"Man." He smiled at me. "This feels so good."

And he began to move, pulling it almost completely out, then plunging it back in to its full depth. I looked at him, watching this beautiful young boy-man as his arms and chest and abs flexed with every movement, his face reddening as he focused on what he was doing. He was sweating again, beads of water forming at his hair line, in the cleavage splitting his chest.

"Oh yeah," I gasped out, and I wanted him inside me, I wanted to take all of him inside me, I wanted to be filled by his body. I started moving against him so that each thrust went deeper into me, so that my body was slamming against his as hard as his was ramming into mine. I reached up and pinched his nipples hard. His breath was coming faster, and when I pinched the nipples again he moaned.

"Oh yeah, baby, that's nice," he panted, smiling down at me, sweat dripping off his nose onto my stomach.

It felt so damned good.

Jason could go to hell.

"Fuck me," I said, reaching up and punching him in the chest slightly. He looked surprised, then grinned. He punched me back in the chest. He leaned down and pressed his mouth against mine, still moving his hips, still fucking, but not as deep. His kiss was hard, strong, as though he were trying to devour me. I grabbed some of his hair and pulled his head back.

He grinned.

He pushed himself back up on his arms and began pounding away again. This time I did scream, giving into the feeling, letting myself go as I never had with Jason, giving in to the animalistic aspects of getting fucked by this hot young man-boy with the big dick, and lifted my legs up, making it easier for him to pound my ass, to take it for his, to lay claim to it and own it, I wanted him to make me his bitch, his whore, his hole, his pig, his tramp, his slut...

"FUCK ME, BOY!" I screamed.

The bed was shaking, the headboard banging against the wall. A picture fell, the glass breaking, but I didn't care, he was taking me, riding me, driving me, pounding me, and it was going to be soon, I closed my eyes and felt the orgasm building inside me, it felt so good.

I screamed as I came, breath coming in gasps, my entire body shivering, my eyes rolling back up in my head, and still he kept fucking me.

He kept fucking.

I was trying to catch my breath and couldn't.

I opened my eyes.

His eyes were closed. His teeth were gritted in determination. Every muscle in his body was flexed, standing out in bas-relief.

I was going to come again.

Sweat dripped off his nose onto my chest.

His entire body went rigid.

He groaned.

I felt my second orgasm start.

He drove deep inside me, his ass clenched, letting out a low shout with each convulsion.

My entire body shook as my own come rained up onto my torso.

We lay like that, his cock still inside me, for a few moments after we both finished.

He wiped sweat out of his eyes and grinned down at me. "Wow."

I smiled back at him. "Yeah. Wow."

I pointed out the bathroom and told him where the towels were. After a few moments, I heard the shower water running.

*My God*, I thought. *My God, my God.*

I knew what I had to do.

I picked up the phone and dialed Jason's office. "Hey, Jason. What time are you going to be home? We really need to talk."

## THE SOUND OF A SOUL CRYING

The dream was mild at first, hardly remembered upon awakening—a vague flash of a blond man in a pair of tight underwear, wrapped in a blanket of a multicolored wool, almost like a serape, but that flash brought with it a sense of unease, discomfort, that horrible gut feeling something was wrong. Galen sat up in the bed, the slight breeze coming from the ceiling fan tousling his light brown hair, rubbing his eyes. He glanced over at the clock. Just before four. He tried for a moment to recapture the dream, the image, but it was just that—an image, nothing more. *Not again*, he thought to himself, getting out of bed to get a drink of water. The last time had been too painful, too hard on him. It had taken weeks to get over. He couldn't afford that again. He took a couple of aspirins as well. There was no headache this time, but it never hurt to be careful.

The second night there was more. This time he got more of a picture of what the blond man looked like: thick blond hair parted in the center, perfectly straight, bleached whiter by sun exposure. His skin was tanned bronze-gold, his lips a thin, almost austere line across his lower face above a slightly pointed jaw. The nose was long, but not too long to offset the rest of his face. The eyes were small, frosted with white lashes and crowned with two white brows. Their color was a dark blue, almost azure. His slender neck connected with heavily muscled shoulders, descending to a hairless chest hardened and rounded with developed muscles. He was wearing navy blue cotton sweatpants that hung loosely off his waist, revealing the two lines where his hips intersected the torso. Slight lines around his eyes and lips betrayed his age to be most likely his early to mid-forties. His face looked as though it had forgotten how to smile. He was watching a video on his television, the remote in his long-fingered hand. He pressed the FF button, and Galen's view of the scene rotated as though a movie camera on a track was moving around, so that his line of sight was behind the couch the man sat on and he could see the blurred images moving quickly by, images of three naked young men with low body fat and veined muscles, erect cocks, one getting fucked while sucking the third's cock. The blond was massaging his crotch, but nothing was happening, there was no physical reaction at all. He finally stopped the tape, turned off the television, and walked into a bedroom. He dropped the sweatpants, revealing a tight pair of thirty-five-dollar white briefs. He slid beneath the multicolored blanket and turned off the light, lying there staring at the ceiling in the darkness.

This time Galen woke with a headache. It wasn't the worst he'd ever had after such a dream, but it wasn't a pleasant one. There was a dull aching throb in his forehead over his right eye, close to the bridge of his nose. He just lay there, his breath coming faster and faster as he focused on the pain, trying to will it away. He got out of the bed to head into the bathroom, his erection poking out from beneath the elastic waistband. The dreams always had that effect; headache and hard-on, two things most people would ordinarily consider mutually exclusive. He shook two aspirins out, popped them into his mouth, and cupped his hands under the faucet for water to wash them down with. He stared at himself in the mirror. The bags under his eyes were getting thicker, darker, larger. The whites of his eyes were laced with red lines, and even the white was starting to look yellowed and tired. He splashed water on his face. *It's only going to get worse, so stop bitching about it now*, he told his reflection, *now is the easy part*. He prayed for the aspirin to work its mysterious magic and got back into the bed.

"It's happening again, isn't it?" his nurse, Bonnie Fontenot, asked him the next morning as they waited for their first patient to arrive.

All he could do was nod, and she patted his arm with sympathy. Bonnie was the only person he had ever confided in about the dreams. She believed in his dreams, she believed in tarot cards and reading tea leaves, in lighting candles to saints and powers beyond anything that science could explain. "You should try those pills Dr. Williams gave you," she went on. "They might work."

He nodded, knowing the pills would stay in the medicine cabinet. She didn't understand, couldn't begin to. He wasn't even sure there was a way he could explain it so that she would. He couldn't understand it himself. He just knew, somehow, the people in his dreams were real people. Real people who were hurting, suffering, in pain. Somehow, his dreaming about them helped them, he was positive about that, although he couldn't have said why, it was just a feeling he had, a feeling once he had the final and most vivid and draining and painful dream about them, that somehow they became better. And if the pills allowed him to fall into a deep sleep, a painless, undisturbed sleep, something bad would happen to those people. So having the dreams was a small price to pay.

Hadn't he become a doctor in order to help people?

That night the dream became even more alive. More of his senses became involved. He could smell the blond now, sense the vibration of his movements on his skin even though the amount of air he disturbed was minute. Galen could smell the aloe in the lotion as the blond rubbed it into the skin around his eyes and lips with shaking hands, staring into his bathroom mirror, the small lines and wrinkles looking deep as canyons and wide as valleys. Galen could smell the avocado in his hair from the conditioner, the mint from his toothpaste, the cucumber in the bar of soap. He could even smell the slight hint of sweat and musk from under the blond's arms, the blond hairs bunched together in moist clumps. Galen could almost feel the velvety smoothness of his skin as he brushed close to the suffering blond man, the coolness of the cotton underwear stretched across his hard muscled ass, the slight static from golden white hairs on his tanned legs. The blond stopped rubbing, his head tilting slightly to one side.

*He senses me*, Galen thought. Sometimes they did, somehow, from some deep instinct or sense from deep inside, some forgotten instinct or ability from the distant past when man lived in caves, cowering from the unknowns out in the dark. That usually meant it was the last dream; however Galen was meant to help, it was finished.

The headache this time was major; it felt like someone had driven an icepick between his eyes and was shaking it around, jolting it back and forth to deepen and widen the wound. As he staggered to the bathroom, a wet sticky spot on his underwear brushed against his skin. His dick ached, and when he looked down he saw a long sticky string of come hanging off the end of it. Yes, he thought as he shook four aspirins into his shaking palm, this was the last time he'd dream of the blond.

As he drove home from work the next night, every muscle aching and his eyes so tired they were burning, he was stopped at the light at the intersection of St. Charles and Poydras. Bored, he looked out the car window to his right where several people were waiting for the streetcar. He shook his head, closed and reopened his eyes.

It couldn't be.

The blond was standing there, wearing a black silk suit, a gray shirt and a red tie, talking into a cell phone. His lips were moving fast, his tanned face flushed. He stopped, shaking his head, opened his mouth and closed it several times, unable to get a word into the conversation. Finally, he closed the phone without saying anything else. He slid the phone back into his jacket pocket.

A horn blared behind Galen, and he moved his foot from the brake to the gas.

The blond *was* a real person.

Blood rushed to his head, and he was almost overcome with a kind of ecstasy. He'd *known* the people in his dreams were real people. He didn't understand any of it, why he had the dreams, how they helped the people he dreamed about, but now he knew he had been right. When he got home he flushed the sleeping pills down the toilet. He watched the clock all night, time moving so slowly he almost screamed in frustration. He even considered going to bed early; he was a little tired, after all, even though the aching soreness in his joints from earlier in the day was long gone. He kept waiting for the adrenaline rush from seeing the blond to wear off, leaving him dead on his feet, but it didn't.

Finally, at ten he went to bed.

And didn't dream.

When he woke in the morning, his alarm raging at him, he opened his eyes to see the morning light streaming through the sheer curtains. He wondered, as he mechanically went through his normal morning routine of shaving, showering, brushing his teeth, drinking coffee, and eating a toasted bagel, if the blond was fine now. Was that why there had been no dream? The dreams had done their job and now he was free from them until the next one came along?

Despite the fact the dreams were so hard on him physically, he realized he *wanted* to dream about the blond again. He wanted to know more about him, wanted to see into his life some more. He wondered why he'd dreamed about him in the first place. He wondered if he would see him again on the street.

He wanted to see him again.

On his way home that night, he watched the sidewalks, looking for the blond.

He didn't see him.

That night, he went to sleep thinking about the blond man. He'd thought about him all day, couldn't seem to be able to get him out of his head. At one point, his need for the blond had become so great he'd had to slip into the bathroom at his office, his erection straining against his pants, and sitting on the toilet, closed his eyes and remembered the blond's body, the way his skin felt as he brushed against him, the deep cleavage, the prominent veins in his shoulders. He stroked himself, bringing himself to a quick climax while he imagined himself on top of the blond, holding his legs up in the air and driving his cock deep inside his hard ass, the blond bringing his ass up to meet each thrust, working into a driving rhythm that eventually would bring them both to a massive climax that would make both of their bodies stiffen and convulse with amazingly intense pleasure. As he slid under the covers, his cock was hardening again. He thought about taking care of it again, as he had that afternoon, but finally decided to just try to get some sleep.

He shut his eyes.

The blond was lying in his bed, idly paging through the latest issue of *Vanity Fair*. He looked as though he were waiting for something, anything. Every so often he would stare off into the distance, fixated on a spot on the ceiling. He was on top of the covers, the only clothing a pair of black cotton bikini briefs. He reached down and scratched underneath his balls. He paused, cocking his head from side to side.

"Is someone there?" His voice was raspy, hoarse sounding. He shook his head. "I must be going crazy," he muttered.

Galen reached out his right hand and touched the blond's leg.

The blond's eyes opened wide, his face draining of color.

*He can feel me*, Galen thought, *he can feel my hand on his leg*.

Galen slid his hand up the smooth, hard leg, stopping only when he reached the black underwear.

"Who are you?" the blond whispered, his voice shaking. Underneath the black cotton, his cock was beginning to swell. "What are you?"

"My name is Galen," he heard himself saying.

The blond sat up a little further in the bed. "Galen?"

*He can hear me*, Galen thought. They'd never been able to hear him before; he'd tried to speak to them before, in the past dream cycles; they'd never responded.

"What is your name?" Galen asked, wanting to call him something other than "the blond."

"D-d-danny."

"Don't be afraid, there's no reason to be afraid of me." He leaned forward and brushed his lips against Danny's cheek. Danny turned his face toward him and reached out his right hand.

Galen felt his fingertips brushing against his chest. *I can feel him touching me*, he thought, his mind racing. He reached down and put his hand on Danny's chest, stroking its round hardness, tracing the outline of his small nipple, which hardened. Danny's blue eyes closed, gooseflesh rising on his arms.

"Who are you?" Danny asked without opening his eyes. "What are you?"

Galen didn't answer. He didn't know how to answer. What could he say, how could he explain? Would Danny even know what an empath was?

Danny's hand was still on Galen's chest, stroking it, and then his fingers chanced on the nipple, which he pinched. Galen's eyes closed as a jolt of electricity seemed to rocket through his body, blood rushing down into his cock. Danny twisted and pulled on the nipple, and Galen moaned, it felt so good, it had been so long since someone had touched him, it…

He opened his eyes and could see his reflection in the mirror. "Can you see me now?" he asked.

Danny nodded. "You're beautiful, Galen."

*He can see me, this can't be a dream, I must really be here*, Galen thought, reaching down and kissing Danny's lips. They were hard and firm, and Danny leaned up into the kiss, his lips parting and making way for Galen's tongue. The kiss was more than just a physical link between them; it seemed to open their very souls to each other with a kind of completeness, a power neither of them had ever experienced before. Their hearts seemed to be beating in synch with each other, and Danny was pulling Galen down on top of him, and even their bodies seemed to mold to each other, chest to chest, Danny's legs coming apart as Galen settled in between them, their erections straining against each other as the kiss continued, Galen slipping his tongue inside Danny's mouth, and Danny gently sucking on it, another jolt of electricity going through Galen's body. He let out a low moan.

He didn't want the kiss to end, but Danny leaned his head back, and Danny was licking and nibbling on his neck. His scalp tingled. Danny's left hand came up and started running through his hair, and Danny was gently pulling him down beside him, and they rolled so that they lay side by side, facing each other on the bed.

"Are you real?" Danny whispered again.

"As real as you want me to be."

Danny smiled and licked Galen's right nipple, swirling his tongue around it, nipping it with his teeth, sucking on it. Galen reached down and grabbed Danny's ass with both hands. It was as hard and firm as he imagined it to be; as he squeezed it Danny tightened it for him. He slid his hand beneath the waistband of Danny's underwear, tracing the outline of the crack between the cheeks with his forefinger. Danny's body shuddered, and he found the hole deep inside the mounds of muscle and outlined it with his finger. Danny's back arched and he let out a moan. Galen drew his finger around it again, tapping it a bit, and Danny's body began to tremble a little bit, goose bumps rising on his arms, chest, legs. Danny's body stiffened, from head to toe, and then relaxed. "Oh...my... God..." Danny breathed out the words, "that fucking feels amazing."

Galen leaned down and kissed the base of Danny's throat. Danny's hands came up and grasped his shoulders, then slid down Galen's back, not stopping until they slid under Galen's waistband, cupping his ass. A shiver ran down Galen's spine. He slid his tongue out and moved down Danny's torso, licking his tanned skin, which tasted slightly of salt and dried sweat. When he reached Danny's navel, he flicked his tongue in and out of the small hole, wetting the downy blond hairs around it. He yanked at Danny's underwear, and Danny raised his hips slightly so they slid down, freeing his hard pink cock, a clear drop glistening in the slit in the head. Galen sat back and worked Danny's underwear down the tanned hard legs until Danny kicked them off with his feet. Galen lowered his head down into Danny's crotch, taking his cock into his mouth, licking it as he slid his mouth down its length, opening his throat to take the entire thing inside.

Danny began to tremble again.

Galen worked upward until all that was left in his mouth was the head, which he swirled his tongue around, sliding his mouth down again—it tasted wonderful, all musk and salt and sweat and magic.

He closed his eyes and felt Danny's heartbeat pounding inside his cock. The pulse was racing, thumping, racing more blood into his cock, which seemed to grow stronger and harder with each pulsing beat. He felt a oneness with Danny, as though both of their hearts were pumping in sync together, a singular feeling of oneness with another man he hadn't felt in years.

Danny's eyes were closed, his hands clenching at the bedsheets as Galen slid his mouth up and off him. Galen sat there, just watching him, reveling in his physical beauty, drinking in the smooth tanned body with his eyes.

Danny opened his own eyes and said clearly, "I want you to fuck me."

Galen smiled down at him, bringing his face down and pressing his lips to Danny's firm ones. Danny's tongue slid between Galen's lips, and Galen fastened his mouth on it, sucking it gently. Danny's eyes closed again, a soft humming coming from low in his throat. Finally, Danny pulled his head back. He smiled up at Galen, pushed him gently in the chest, forcing Galen down onto his back.

He rolled off the bed and opened a drawer in his nightstand, pulling out a half-empty bottle of lube and a foil-wrapped condom. Danny popped the lid on the lube, then reached over and slid Galen's underwear down and off. He straddled him, squirting lube out into the palm of his hand, then reaching down and wetting Galen's straining cock, which sprang up harder at the touch. He bit the condom package open, almost frantically rolled the condom down over Galen, wetting Galen's cock again. He grabbed hold of Galen's cock and positioned it as he sat back down.

Galen looked up at him, at the defined abs, the flat slabs of muscle across the chest, the pink cock standing straight up, still moist from the sucking he'd given it, as Danny inserted the tip of Galen's cock into his ass. Danny's eyes were closed in concentration, beads of sweat appearing at his hairline, as he gently, softly, carefully began to settle down on Galen's cock. Unable to resist, Galen slid his hands up Danny's torso until they reached the small nipples perched on an outer fold of pectoral muscle. The nipples were hard as diamonds, and he tweaked each of them. Danny gasped and slid down another inch before stopping with a gasp.

"Oh…my…God…" Danny's voice came out in an urgent whisper. "This is fucking amazing, man, oh man, oh, man…" His breath came in quicker gasps as he settled further down, getting about halfway down Galen's shaft when he gasped and moaned again, stopping and sliding up a tiny, almost imperceptible bit, his entire body going momentarily rigid.

Galen closed his own eyes, feeling the tight pressure on the upper half of his cock, resisting the urge to force his hips upward, to drive it completely in, to fill Danny with his hardness, to feel that silky smoothness gripping his entire cock, his balls almost aching from the need to slap up against Danny's hard muscled ass.

He became aware of his own heartbeat, almost thundering in his ears, Danny's echoing it, both of their breathing coming faster, in desperate little gasps.

Danny took a deep breath and slid all the way down.

A low growl came from deep inside Danny as he settled down onto Galen's body. His head went back, exposing the veins in his throat. Beads of sweat glistened on his torso as he slid up, then back down slowly, rocking. Their bodies found a rhythm of their own, a rhythm instinctual, free of restraint, as if they were playing a piece of music on each other, a duet of sweat, passion and pleasure. Galen watched as Danny's body worked on his cock, up and down, rocking back and forth when it reached the base of Galen's cock, grinding gently, the pressure in his own balls building.

And then with a gasp Danny was coming, short cries of ecstasy escaping through his pursed lips as the hot white drops sprayed out onto Galen's chest, and Galen felt his own eruption start, his body stiffening with an intensity he'd never felt before, his eyes rolling back in his head as he convulsed, his body lurching upward with each release...

He sat up in bed with a start, his own bed. The alarm was ringing. Sunlight was streaming through the louvered blinds on the windows. The luminous numbers on the clock read seven a.m.

He rubbed his eyes. A dream? Could that intensity have merely been a dream?

He got out of the bed. There was no headache this time. His balls ached a bit. He went into the shower and got ready for another day of work.

The day passed in a blur of patients, examinations,

inoculations, and prescriptions. He left the office at five thirty and on his way home decided to stop for a drink. He did this every so often on a Friday, needing an escape. He parked on Dauphine Street and walked over a block to the Pub. He ordered a vodka and cranberry, and sat at one of the tall tables in the corner, in the shadows, and turned his eyes up to the video screen, playing the latest Kylie Minogue dance hit.

"This is going to sound weird, but I've been dreaming about you."

Galen turned, and there was Danny, standing next to his table, wearing a black tank top and a skintight pair of faded blue jeans. He was holding a vodka tonic in his right hand while the other was twisting and shredding a napkin.

"It doesn't sound weird at all, actually," Galen heard himself saying. "I've been dreaming about you, too."

Danny smiled, a smile that lit up his eyes, relaxing tension lines from around his eyes. "Have we, um, ever met before?"

Galen shook his head. "I don't think so."

"Is your name Galen?"

Galen nodded. "And you're Danny."

Danny pulled up a bar stool and sat down across from him. "So."

Galen smiled. "So."

Danny flushed. "The dreams I've been having—well, they were kind of intense."

Galen reached over and took his hand. "Let's not talk about the dreams, okay? I'd rather talk about the reality."

Danny smiled and nodded.

So began the slow process of getting to know each other.

## The Sea Where It's Shallow

They weren't happy.
I could tell.

The couple was sitting on beach towels a few feet beyond where the lapping of the waves at the sand turned it a darker hue than where it was dry. One was blond, the other brunette. The blond was older, maybe by as few as five years, maybe as many as ten. The brunette was taller by about four inches, but the blond was stockier, with thicker muscles.

I crossed the line from where the depth of the water changes, where it switches from blue to green. I'd been swimming a long time, and perhaps it was time to come out. This couple definitely needed me, my intervention. Their auras were all wrong. They loved each other but something was going on with them, something that was making them forget how much they loved, how much they cared, how deep the feelings actually ran. The brunette was scowling. They weren't speaking, merely sitting side by side on their individual blankets on the powdery white sand. Not even looking at each other, not even stealing the occasional sidelong glance.

My feet brushed against the bottom and I smiled. I'd been in the water long enough, it seemed, to forget how to walk. Okay, maybe that was an exaggeration. I hoped not, at any rate. My feet sank a fraction of an inch into the sand, and the small waves lifted the weight off my feet momentarily as each one passed, moving me a little closer to the water's edge.

I kept my eyes on the brunette as more of me emerged from the water. He tried to make it look like he wasn't looking at me. I was getting the sideling glances as his eyes scanned the horizon, but they always came back to me. He seemed afraid to look me in the eyes, for our gazes to lock, but his eyes, I could see them moving, drinking in every inch of my dripping body as it emerged from the green sea. The white sugary sand of the Florida panhandle scrunched under my feet as I walked at last out of the water. I smiled at the brunette. The blond had lain back, sunglasses on, his eyes unreadable. The brunette was more susceptible to my charms, I decided, sitting down on the sand a few feet from where he sat.

I would wait a few minutes, letting the sun dry my skin, I decided, giving him the opportunity to speak first. Unless I missed my guess, he would.

The sun's rays were warm, and my skin dried quickly in its glare. I sensed him there, wanting to speak, to open a dialogue, but afraid of how the blond would react.

Fair enough.

I turned my head and looked right into his brown eyes. He looked away quickly, his tanned face coloring slightly, embarrassed at being caught looking. "Hello," I said, rearranging my facial muscles into a smile. It felt awkward. Surely it hadn't been that long since I'd smiled? For a brief moment, I tried to recall the last time.

"Um, hi." He looked back at me. He really had a pretty face, the skin still soft and supple with the last fading glow of youth. Late twenties, I decided. His eyes were beautiful in their brownness, golden flecks lightening them just slightly enough to make them different from the many others with the same eye coloring. His lashes were long, thick, black, curling up and away from the lids. Deep dimples appeared in his cheeks as his red lips spread across his face in a slightly shy smile. Large, white, straight, even teeth appeared over the cleft in his chin. His skin was olive, the kind that tans deeply and easily. Black curly hair framed his face, and below it a graceful neck reached down into powerful shoulders. There was a patch of curly hair between widely set pectorals, which trailed down over a flat stomach before disappearing into the white Lycra of his bikini. "My name's Matt."

I inclined my head down a bit, closing my eyes. "Alexandros." I could sense the blond's eyes on us behind his sunglasses. There was no expression on his face, but the muscles in his neck tightened.

Matt made a gesture at him. "This is my partner, Chris."

*Who feels threatened*, I thought. Matt was still smiling at me. "A pleasure, Chris," I said, inclining my head at him. Chris pulled himself up till he was reclining on his elbows. His torso was hairless, thickly muscled.

"Alexander, did you say?" He lifted his sunglasses to look at me in the bright glare. His eyes were gray. He glanced up and down my body.

"Alexandros," I corrected him softly. "Call me Sandy."

"You swim a lot?" His skin gleamed in the sunlight, a mixture of suntan oil and sweat shining in the bright sun.

"Yes."

His eyes flickered down again before meeting mine. "It shows." He got to his feet. His legs were thick with muscle. He wasn't as tall as I originally had thought, maybe five eight or nine. His black bikini had ridden up a bit in the back, revealing pale skin on his round hard ass. "I think I'll go for a swim myself."

Both Matt and I watched him as he walked down to the waterline, wading out. Once he was in deep enough water, he dove under the surface and started swimming. I turned back to Matt. "He's quite beautiful," I said.

"Yes." A shadow passed over Matt's face, lifting as he smiled at me. "So are you."

"Thank you," I replied. "You are, as well. You make quite a striking couple."

Matt looked away from me, up the beach. "Thanks."

"How long have you been together?"

"Three years."

*Three years—that could explain some of it*, I thought. The bloom is now off the rose. The first year is all giddy with love and sexual exploration of each other. In the second year the passion starts to die, just a little bit. The third year is the tricky one, when eyes start to wander, when the sex becomes a little stale and boring. Little things that used to be dismissed now begin to rankle just a little, simmering beneath the surface. "And it's going well?"

"Well—" Matt made a gesture with his hands. "Things are changing a bit. I don't know if it's a good or a bad thing. I mean, I still love him, and I think he still loves me, but things just aren't the way they used to be."

"Ah."

"We met in a bar, of all places," Matt went on. "I was out with some friends, celebrating my birthday. I saw him standing in a corner, by himself. He really took my breath away when I looked at him." He closed his eyes. "He was so gorgeous and sexy—the kind of guy I'd always wanted but could never get."

"Really?"

He looked at me, his eyes sad. "I was different then, Sandy. I didn't work out—I hadn't set foot in a gym since high school. I was pretty overweight, kind of dumpy. One of my friends noticed me staring at him, and he went over to Chris."

He laughed. "He told Chris that it was my birthday and he wanted Chris to be my birthday present. Chris went along with it and came over. We started talking, and I went home with him." He sighed. "It was pretty amazing, and then he actually called me and asked me out again. I was crazy about him, and after a few months I moved in with him. He got me to join his gym, and he put me on a program." He gestured to his body. "And this is the result."

"You look great."

"Yeah." He stared out at the water. Chris was a small dot out in the distance. "I look great. So why doesn't Chris want me anymore?"

There it was, the root of the problem. "He doesn't?"

"No." A tall, lean young man of about twenty with deeply bronzed skin wearing long baggy yellow shorts walked by at the water line. We both watched him for a moment, and Matt looked back at me. "I mean, when I was fat we had sex all the time. Every day. He couldn't get enough of me—but the better shape I got in, the less sex we had. Now I look better than I ever have, good enough for total strangers to hit on me, and Chris can't be bothered with me, unless we have someone else with us, a three-way. And even then, Chris is more into the other guy than he is me." He shrugged. "I mean, he was the one who wanted me to work out. Why would he do that if he liked me better when I was fat?"

"It doesn't make sense to me." I shrugged back at him. "Have you talked to him about it?"

"No."

"Ah."

Matt looked out at the water. "You see, he took the swim so we could talk. When he gets back, the first thing he'll do is ask me what I think, and if I nod, he'll ask you back to our room for a drink. At some point during the walk back, he'll say to you 'I can't wait to watch Matt fuck you.' If you're open to it—" He shrugged again.

"Is that what you want, Matt?"

He smiled then, a big smile that lit up his entire face. "You're pretty hot, Sandy. Yeah, I would really like to fuck you."

"But you'd rather fuck Chris."

The smile faded. "Yeah."

We sat in silence as Chris became bigger and bigger as he swam to shore. He emerged from the sea, salty water streaming off his body. He shook his head, sending water droplets flying in all directions from his hair. He walked toward us. He looked at Matt. "What do you think?"

I saw the pain briefly flash across Matt's face before he lowered his head and nodded. An odd look went across Chris's face as he turned to me and smiled. "Would you like to come back to our room for a drink?"

I looked him square in those murky gray eyes. "Only if the drink is a preliminary to fucking."

He was startled, but only for a moment, and he smiled. "Whatever you want, Sandy."

It took them a few moments to fold their towels, pack up their stuff, and then we were walking across the hot sand. Matt walked faster than Chris and I. Chris reached over and stroked my back. "You really have a great body," he whispered. "I can't wait to see Matt fuck you."

I smiled back at him. "But you'll be joining us, won't you?"

His face lit up with a smile that told me everything I needed to know. It was so clear, so obvious, but of course Matt, wrapped up in his insecurities, couldn't know, couldn't notice, didn't see it. To him, Chris was perfect, the perfect man, the perfect lover, everything he had ever wanted. How could Chris be insecure? Chris draped his arm around my shoulders. I looked deep into his eyes and saw things that had never occurred to Matt. Chris was older. The age difference was even greater than I originally thought. Chris was forty, Matt only twenty-seven. He looked at Matt and saw an incredibly beautiful younger man with his whole life in front of him. Matt had been fat and shy when they met.

Chris was expecting Matt to find someone younger and prettier and leave him.

He had no idea how much Matt loved him.

Neither one of them could really see.

Their room was actually a suite on one of the upper floors of their hotel. One wall was all glass and faced the sea. Once we were inside, Matt took a shower to wash the oil and sweat off. Chris poured himself a gin and tonic and me a glass of water. He walked over to the glass wall and stared out at the sea.

"You think he's going to leave you."

He turned back to me, and I could see the pain in his eyes. He shrugged. "He's young and he's beautiful. I'm getting old. You do the math."

As though forty was the end.

"You think he loves you as little as that?"

The sound of the shower stopped. He smiled at me. "My turn."

Matt came out, wearing a large white towel wrapped around his waist. Chris passed him without a word, without a touch. Matt looked after him, and then at me. He smiled at me and shrugged. He walked over to where I was sitting in a wingback chair and pulled me to my feet. He touched my chest with one hand and his other came around the back, squeezing my ass. His erection loosened the towel and it fell off. His cock was long, hard and thick, springing out from a small patch of trimmed black pubic hair. He slipped a hand into my bikini, fingers exploring the gulley in the center. I reached down and slid it down and off me. "Wow," he said, looking down momentarily.

"Let's wait for Chris."

He nodded and pulled me over to the bed. We climbed on top of it, side by side, and started kissing. He was a wonderful kisser. Our tongues explored the inside of each other's mouths. I was getting aroused, how could I not? I wanted to feel that big thick cock inside me. I heard the shower turn off and we kept kissing, softly, gently. Out of the corner of my eye I saw Chris walk back into the room, naked, toweling off his back. He looked at us, his eyes somewhat downcast, and sat down in the wingback chair I had vacated.

I pulled my head away from the kissing and looked at Chris. His eyes were full of pain. I could see it. *Is Sandy the one*, he was asking himself, *the elusive one out there Matt will leave me for?*

Such amazing stupidity, such blindness.

I held out my hand toward him and beckoned him to join us.

He smiled almost gratefully, and walked over to the bed. He took my hand and climbed up with us, his own cock springing to life. He was almost as big as Matt, but where Matt's had a huge head and stayed thick all the way down, Chris's cock had a small head at the top, growing thicker and longer as it reached back into his magnificent body. He brought his mouth down to my right nipple and began teasing it with his tongue.

My body immediately responded, a moan escaping my lips and my back arching slightly. When Matt saw what stimulated this response, he lowered his mouth to my left nipple and began doing the same.

My entire body went rigid, my breath coming in gasps.

I reached down with both hands, taking a thick cock in each hand, and began to massage them, my hands moving up and down.

Moans escaped each of them.

Their mouths began exploring my body, lips and tongues moving down and about my torso.

Chris reached into a bag and pulled out a bottle of lube. He squirted some onto his cock, some onto Matt's, and some onto mine. I continued rubbing their cocks, only now my hands were more slippery, gliding along the skin, sliding over the heads.

"I want to fuck you," Matt whispered.

I looked up at Chris. Lust blazed in his eyes, and he nodded. I turned myself over onto my stomach, arching my back, lifting my ass up into the air. Matt moved down behind me. Chris opened a condom and handed it to Matt. Chris positioned himself in front of me, my head between his legs. That big tapering cock was right in front of me. He wiped the lube off with a towel. I felt exploratory fingers probing me. I shuddered. I flicked my tongue over the head of Chris's beautiful cock.

I gasped and flinched as Matt moved inside me.

"Slow down, honey," Chris said. To me, he whispered, "He forgets how big he is."

I smiled up at him and began licking his cock again. Chris moaned as Matt began to slide gently inside me. I opened up for him, relaxing the necessary muscles so that he could get there.

He needed to be completely inside me for this to work.

I moaned as I felt his cock slide all the way in.

But before I could do what I needed to do, he slid back out.

I took Chris into my mouth, swirling my tongue around. I took him down, opening my throat, tilting my head back slightly to open the passage. I reached the root and stayed there, waiting, waiting, waiting…

Matt slammed into me from behind.

I opened the portal in my mind.

No matter how many times I have done this, I am never prepared for it, and there certainly is no way to prepare them for it.

The purity of their love for each other flowed through my body, Matt's emotion passing through my mouth into Chris's body, Chris's passing through the other side.

All three of our bodies went completely rigid, every muscle tightening up.

"Oh my God," Chris breathed.

My body was trembling as the love passed through, visions of the two of them together, fucking each other, loving each other, flashing through my brain like a kaleidoscope. Their fears, their doubts, their insecurities. I focused on stopping those feelings from passing through. That wasn't the idea. But it was so difficult because the love itself was so pure, so powerful, so strong that it filled my mind, made me almost forget what I was doing, my purpose here. Wave after wave of pleasure was passing through me, pleasure from the big cock in my ass, the big cock in my mouth, but I had to focus, I had to take the bad away from the two of them, I couldn't fail them, I focused and concentrated on grabbing the impure with my mind; I visualized a suitcase and started shoving those bad emotions into the suitcase, and when there were finally none left, when all that was passing through was purity, I shut the suitcase and closed the portal.

Both Chris and Matt were shuddering.

I pulled my head back from Chris in time as he released a stream of come into my face and hair.

Matt's entire body erupted, convulsed, as his orgasm exploded into the condom.

My own pumped out into the sheets.

Matt withdrew from me and collapsed onto the bed beside me.

I sat up, my chest and stomach covered with my own orgasm.

Chris slid down onto the bed and smiled. "My God."

I stood up. "Mind if I shower?"

They both shook their heads.

The water was hot as I scrubbed my skin clean, washing come out of my hair, off my face, off my chest. I dried myself and walked back into the bedroom, picking up my bikini off the floor, sliding it up my legs, tucking myself back into it.

Matt and Chris were in each other's arms, kissing gently, staring into each other's eyes.

When I reached the door, Chris said, "You don't have to leave."

I turned back to them. "No, I think I do."

"Will we see you again?" Matt asked.

I smiled at them, one dark, the other light. So beautiful together. "Perhaps." I shut the door behind me.

The sand was hot on my feet as I walked back down to the water's edge. My skin was getting dry. I turned and looked back at the hotel, finding their windows. I raised my hand in a salute, although I doubted they were watching. I walked into the water, the warm, welcoming green water of the gulf. When

I reached waist level, I started to swim. At the line where the water turns blue, I dived to the bottom. No need for the crowd of sunbathers to see what was going to happen. I thrust through the water and felt the gills starting to open again on the side of my throat. My legs came together, the skin meeting in the center and starting to knit. I pointed my toes and the fin began to form.

I swam out to sea.

## UNSENT

*Dear Todd,*

 *I hope you don't mind I'm writing this letter. You said you didn't mind, so I'm guessing you don't.*

 *I wanted to thank you for being such a nice guy... it's funny, I've been wanting to write this letter for a long time; I started writing you so many times and I just ended up throwing the letters away every time. I know you probably think I'm just a goof; a dumb kid who doesn't know what he wants or needs or anything, and that's true, I guess. I don't know what I want to do with my life...if I live through this. I just wanted to fly planes, and now I am flying them...but this is different.*

 *I guess I was just naïve and stupid when I joined the Air Force. All I wanted to do was fly planes...it never occurred to me I'd be flying planes and killing people...pretty dumb, right?*

❖

He was just a boy.

*He can't be more than fifteen* was my first thought when he walked into Lafitte's that Tuesday morning. There was no one in the bar besides me; it was only twelve thirty. I was working the five a.m. till one shift, covering for Mike. This shift sucked. The only hope to make any kind of money was leftovers from the previous night when you start, and they're gone by nine…so for the last four hours of the shift it was just me and the cleaning women, and they were gone by eleven.

He stood for a few seconds in the doorway, hesitating. I looked up from wiping down the bar for the thousandth time in the last twenty minutes and smiled to myself. I recognized the hesitation—an underage kid steeling his nerve to sit at the bar and ask for a drink. *Well, kid,* I said to myself, *prepare to be carded.*

He walked in and sat down on a bar stool right in front of me. He was cute, still with a little baby fat in his pale, freckled face. His hair was military buzzed, reddish blond, and his eyes gray. He was wearing a red sweater and a pair of blue jeans.

I put my rag away under the bar. "What can I do for you?" I asked.

He looked around the bar, not meeting my eyes. "A beer?"

"You got ID?"

He reached into his back pocket and pulled out a worn black wallet, pulling out a military ID, which he slid across the bar to me. I picked it up. The picture was him, all right, looking maybe ten years old, innocent and young. The birthdate was August 12, 1968. Yeah, well, so I was wrong about his age. "What kind of beer? A draft?"

"Yeah." He nodded and smiled at me. His whole face lit up when he smiled, his full lips pulling back over slightly crooked, yellowed teeth. I got a plastic cup and filled it at the tap, my back to him. I placed it on a napkin. "Dollar fifty."

He handed me two ones, and I gave him his change. He

left the quarters on the bar, and I slid them into my hand and tossed them into my tip bucket. "Not very busy, huh?" he said, looking down at the bar, not touching the beer.

I shrugged. "Nah, we're never busy—don't even know why we bother being open."

"Yeah." He toyed with his napkin. "Do you mind talking to me? I don't wanna be a bother."

I laughed and gestured to the empty bar. "Not like I got anything else to do."

He smiled again. "Good." He sipped the beer, looking down at the bar again.

"Where you from?" Standard New Orleans bartender opening—when in doubt, ask where they're from.

"Laurel." Mississippi—that explained the sweet accent.

"What's your name?" I held my hand out over the bar. "I'm Todd."

"Tommy." He shook my hand. His grip was strong, sure, even though the palm was moist.

"What brings you to town?"

"I'm flying out tomorrow morning." He looked down again. "Going back from leave."

Ah, the military. "What branch?" My stomach dropped a little bit. Saddam Hussein had invaded Kuwait, and the world stood on the brink of a war.

"Air Force."

"You fly jets?" I grinned at him, leaning on the bar.

He grinned shyly back at me. "Yeah."

"You going over there?"

He nodded, his smile fading. "Yeah."

I didn't know what to say. I just stood there, looking into his sad gray eyes. Finally, I said, "You'll be okay." It sounded lame to me.

"Thanks." He laughed. It was a sweet sound, boyish, the

kind of laughter you heard in the locker room after a football game. "'preciate that, man." He looked around the bar again. "I've walked by here so many times before but never had the nerve to come in." He shrugged. "And now, I figured, what the hell, right? I might die over there, so what could it hurt? And no one's here."

❖

*I think about dying all the time. All of us over here do, even though we don't talk about it. It's like the Grim Reaper is always outside our tents, you know what I mean? So we play cards and watch some television and write letters and read books, trying to take our minds off what we are going to have to do... the risks we'll be taking. I write my mama, I write my sisters and my brothers, but there isn't anyone I can write to and be honest with, you know? I don't want my family to worry...and the only friends I have are my squad, and we can't talk about any of the things I want to talk about...*

❖

He laughed again. "Just my luck, right?"

"Are you gay?" I couldn't believe I'd said it, after the words had come out.

He looked at me for a long time, our eyes locked. I wondered if he was going to slug me, get mad and storm out of the bar. He smiled, the corners of his mouth turning up in a shy way, and his eyes went down again. "Yeah, I think so," he half whispered. "I joined the Air Force 'cause I thought it'd make a man out of me."

I looked at his boyish face and tried to remember what it was like for me at that age, my first time in a gay bar, how nervous but exhilarated I'd been, how disappointed I would have been had I been the only person there. I didn't know what to say.

"Guess it didn't work." He sighed, shredding the edges of his napkin. "You know, I try. I go out with my squad to bars and meet women...but I just don't feel anything for them, you know what I mean?" He laughed. "All the other guys think I'm this heartbreaker stud because I don't ever want a girlfriend, just keep playing the field, but..." His voice trailed off and he looked down into his beer again. "I didn't tell my mom I was shipping out tomorrow...I told her it was today. I decided to come down to New Orleans and spend the day here...and maybe..." He shrugged. He looked back up at me and smiled. "Thanks for talking to me."

"You know, I get off work here in about half an hour." I don't know why I said it. He'd gotten to me in some way. "I'd be happy to show you around."

His smile was adorable. "Really, I just want to spend some time with someone. I don't care about going to bars or whatever. I just don't want to be alone today." His voice broke momentarily, he swallowed and looked down. "I really don't want to be alone."

I put my hand on his. "Okay, Tommy."

❖

*I feel so alone here. The guys play cards and read their letters from home out loud, you know, just trying to kill time until we get orders to start. The desert is kind of pretty...it's like a long beach where you can't see the water. At night you can see all the stars...and*

*I look up and wonder if you're looking at the same
stars on the other side of the world, and I wonder
what I'm doing here...what's a boy from a small
town in Mississippi doing halfway around the world?
I shouldn't be here, I don't belong here...but then I
never belonged anywhere. I love my mom, I love my
family, but I never belonged in Laurel...part of why I
joined the Air Force was to belong somewhere...but
this didn't take either. I never really knew what to do
with my life...and now I wonder if I've made some
big mistake...maybe I should have just moved to New
Orleans or Atlanta or someplace...San Francisco
or New York...somewhere where it would have been
okay for me to be myself...*

❖

After I got off work, we went back to my apartment so I
could take a shower and make some coffee. I wasn't a morning
person, never have been, and I was tired. All morning long I'd
been waiting to get off work so I could go home and go back to
sleep, but now I couldn't. There was just something about him,
I couldn't quite put my finger on it, but I wanted to take care
of him. After I got cleaned up and changed my clothes, we sat
in my little kitchen and drank coffee, and he told me about his
life growing up. His daddy had died when he was only ten, and
his mama had to support him and his brother and two sisters.
It was hard, there was no chance for college for him, and he
wanted to get out of Laurel, wanted to be a man, wanted to be
what he was supposed to be. He'd liked the Air Force, he liked
his squad, but he listened to them talk about fags and queers
contemptuously, and knew they'd turn against him if they

knew. So he went with them to bars and picked up women, joined them in talking about pussy and tits and fucking.

"Have you ever been with another man?" I asked finally.

He sipped at his coffee. "No."

"Do you want to be with me?"

He looked down. "I'd like that, very much."

❖

*...but then I think about what it would do to Mama, if she knew, and how hard it would be for her in Laurel if anyone else ever found out...and I wonder if I made the right choice...sitting here at night listening to the wind and looking at the stars, I can't help but feel I made the wrong decisions, every step of the way. All I've ever wanted was to be loved, and to love someone else, to have what Mama had with Daddy...can two men have that kind of love? I'd like to believe so... and I've realized that it would be wrong for me to keep living this lie, to marry some woman and have children, all the while wanting to be with another man...*

❖

I undressed him.

He kept trembling as I pulled the sweater over his head. His skin was pale, his shoulders speckled with freckles. His body was lean and hard, his nipples round and pink on the hard muscles of his chest. I held him as he trembled, my bare chest against his, and then we kissed, his mouth tasting of cigarettes and coffee, but still somehow sweet. I took him by the hand and led him over to my bed. He took his boots off, and then I undid his pants, sliding them down over pale muscled legs covered with thick blond hair, and then his white Hanes underwear came off. His cock was long but thin, pinkish and hard. I pushed against his chest gently until he sat back down on the bed. I undressed and sat down next to him.

"Are you sure you want to do this?" I whispered to him.

He swallowed and nodded.

I began kissing his neck, moving my lips down to his right nipple, which I licked and sucked on. He groaned, his whole body going rigid, then trembling. I hugged him tightly, began working on his hard cock. He was just a boy, after all, and he came almost immediately, but stayed hard.

Ah, youth.

❖

*...so I've made up my mind. When my time comes up for reeinlisting this fall, I am going to leave the service. I'm going to come back to New Orleans, and maybe go to the university on the GI Bill. I've saved up almost all my money since I've been in, and I think it's the right thing to do.*

*And I'm going to tell Mama the truth, even if it hurts her, because I love her and want her to love me for who I am, not for who she thinks I am...*

❖

We made love together the rest of the afternoon, never leaving my apartment. We ordered dinner in, and we just held each other for most of the time. He told me about his hopes and his dreams, and how scared he was of the coming conflict.

He slept in my arms that night, holding on to me like a baby with a teddy bear.

In the morning, I called him a cab to take him to the airport.

"Do you mind if I write to you?" he asked. "I don't really have anyone I can write to…it would mean a lot to me."

"Of course you can." I wrote my name and address down for him, and he folded it carefully and placed it in his wallet.

I walked him to the door. The cab was waiting out front. He wrapped his arms around me and held on to me like a lifeline, and then he smiled and walked out the door and got into the cab.

❖

*…I think about you all of the time. Whenever things get rough, or I get scared, I remember the way you held me that last night, how sweet you were, how kind, and I don't know, Todd, maybe I'm in love with you…I close my eyes and I can see your smile, and remember the way you touched me so gently, like you were afraid I'd break or something, and it gets me through…part of the reason I want to come back to New Orleans is to see you again…I miss you all of the time…do you think there's a chance we might be able to be together? That's what I hold on to, what I'll hold on to through everything that's coming. Whenever I get scared I think of you…*

❖

The months passed, and Kuwait was free. Like everyone else, I watched CNN every chance I got while I went about the business of living my life, of getting up and going to work and slinging cocktails, going to bars and meeting men. And sometimes, when they were hurriedly throwing their clothes back on and getting out of my apartment as quickly as they could, I remembered a sweet little boy from Mississippi who'd wanted to stay and held on to me as hard as he could, who didn't want to leave.

And I said a little prayer for him.

❖

*...it's been really hard for me to write this letter. My friends are always bothering me about it, because I won't let them see it, won't tell them who I'm writing to, and they all think I've finally found a woman to love...they've noticed the difference in me and they tease me about it. If they only knew...it kills me not to be able to share this with anyone but you...*

*Todd, do you think you could love me?*

❖

It was a beautiful May morning. The weather had started getting hot and sticky again, and my air conditioner was running 24/7 to keep the damp out of my apartment. It was my day off, a Thursday, and I was going to stay home and clean the place. I'd really been bad, letting the laundry go, not cleaning or doing anything I should, and I'd finally had enough.

I was sorting the laundry into big piles on the living room floor when someone rang my doorbell. I walked over and peeked through the curtains, and saw a short woman I didn't recognize. I opened the door. "May I help you?"

"Are you Todd Gregory?" she asked. She was maybe

five feet tall, wearing a black sweater and black stretch pants. She was overweight, maybe in her late forties, and she looked tired—her eyes were red and watery. She was wearing too much makeup and her thick hair was dyed black, but she'd probably been pretty when she was younger. Her accent was thick.

"Um, yes."

"I'm Ila Mae Harper." She looked into my face. "Tommy's mother."

At first I didn't know what she was talking about, and then I remembered my little Air Force pilot from so many months before. My heart sank. The last thing I needed was a confrontation with his mother. I invited her to come in, apologizing for the mess, and cleared a space on the couch for her to sit, offering her coffee, anything, wondering how to avoid this, how to get her out of there.

She clutched her black patent leather purse as though for dear life as she looked around my apartment. She smiled weakly. "Thank you, but no, I don't need nothing. I just want to talk to you for a minute."

I heard Tommy's voice echoing in my head. "Is he okay?" I asked, and once the words left my mouth, I knew.

Her eyes filled. "Tommy was shot down over Baghdad." For a moment she was overcome, but she got control again.

I felt like I'd been punched in the stomach. I just stared at her in shock.

She was opening her purse. She pulled out an envelope and held on to it, staring down at it. She took a deep breath. "When the Air Force sent me his things, this was in them." She held it out to me.

I took it from her. My name and address were scrawled on the face of the envelope. It was fairly thick. I just stared at it.

"I—I'm sorry, but I read it…" She swallowed. "I want you

to know I loved my son. He was my baby, my first. Nothing would have changed that." She wiped at her face. "It breaks my heart that he felt, that he could have possibly thought, anything would have changed that. Since I—" Her voice broke, and she looked away from me for a moment before continuing. "Since he was killed…" and she started to cry.

I moved over to the couch and took her in my arms. My head was spinning, my stomach lurching. My hands felt cold.

She leaned into me. "Since he was killed, I've wondered what I ever did, how I failed him as a mother that he thought he couldn't tell me the truth. I would have loved him, Mr. Gregory, no matter what…I want you to know that."

"Call me Todd," I said.

She went on as though I hadn't spoken. "And when I think he joined the Air Force because he couldn't…" A sob rose in her throat. Her entire body shook as she sobbed. She stopped, wiping at her mascara-smeared cheeks. "You know, even when he was a little boy, I knew he was special, different, and I loved him all the more because of it. He was just the sweetest little boy, so thoughtful and loving and considerate of other people…everyone just loved him, you know? And when they called me to tell me he was—" She bit her lip. "I thought, when I tried to make sense of it all, that maybe I could sense all along he wasn't meant for this world for long, he was just too good for this world, you know what I mean?"

"Yes." I did know, thinking about a scared but sweet little boy in a man's body, holding him all night long before he went off to war. My own eyes filled.

"Anyway." She got to her feet. "I wanted you to have that letter." She moved toward the front door and I followed her. At the door, she paused, and reached up and kissed my cheek. "Thank you for making my boy happy." Then she was through the door and walking up the street, a brokenhearted little rural woman from Mississippi who might not ever regain the light in her heart.

❖

*So, that's what gives me the strength to get through this all...the chance of seeing you again. I hope you don't mind...but when this is over and I get leave again, I'm going to come see you. I sometimes get scared,and think maybe he won't want to see me again, or maybe he doesn't even remember who I am, but I'm willing to take the risk.*

*I love you, Todd.*

*Tommy*

❖

I cried while I read his letter, as he poured out his heart to me. I cried over what might have been, what could have been, what should have been. I cried for a sweet boy with a thick Mississippi accent wearing blue jeans and a sweater sitting at a bar, shredding a napkin. I cried for the lost potential. I cried for the letter in my hands, never sent, for never having the chance to write him back, to let him know how special he was. In my mind I could see his face in his cockpit, knowing he was going to die. Did he cry, I wondered, as his plane fell out of the sky? Did he think about me?

Were his last thoughts of me?

I lay down in my bed, my laundry forgotten, and I remembered lying there with him in my arms, holding him and kissing the top of his head.

I just lay there, until the sun went down, and then I roused myself and had to get out...to get away. I walked down to

Lafitte's. The bar was empty when I walked in, a few people scattered here and there, the music loud.

And for a second, I saw him sitting there at the end of the bar, and he smiled when he saw me.

But when I reached out my hand to him, he faded away, like he'd never been there.

It's been fourteen years, but I still have his letter, carefully folded in a metal box where I keep things like my high school football letter and medals from track meets I ran a million years ago.

Once a year I drive up to Laurel and lay roses on his grave.

I don't think I'll ever forget that shy, sweet smile.

## MAN IN A SPEEDO

I love you, man in a Speedo.
Yes, I know your real name is actually Jason.
But I always think of you as *man in a Speedo*.
That was what you were wearing the first time I saw you.
And what a sight it was.

It was a Sunday afternoon at the Country Club on Louisa Street, do you remember? It was July, and so fucking hot and humid. I was sitting on one of the lounge chairs on the deck, sipping a vodka tonic out of a perspiring clear plastic cup. I had just sat up to rub some more tanning oil on my chest when you came walking out of the building to the pool area. You were wearing sunglasses, your thick black hair slicked back, a pair of leather sandals and a baggy pair of basketball shorts. Your skin was darkly tanned, Italian-looking with that tint of olive to it, and your body. Oh my God your body. Your pecs were the size of my head, I swear, and those purplish nipples so big and inviting. Your stomach, flat, not defined, like you don't mind eating a bacon cheeseburger every now and again, not like those other arrogant boys who won't eat carbs after seven p.m. or watch every gram of fat that crosses their lips; your muscular legs looking like tree trunks, shaved smooth. I sat there, my mouth open, and you walked to a chair on the other side of the pool, set your bag down, sat down, slipped the sandals off, and then stood up again. You stretched, yawning, your arms and chest flexing, the lats springing out, the curly black hair in your armpits glistening and wet. You reached down and slid the shorts down, revealing a bright yellow bikini that made your tan look even darker. The suit hung off your hips, revealing an amazing pouch in the front. You turned, and stretched again, and I saw your ass, hard and round and muscular, flex inside its yellow Lycra container, which could barely contain it. I could just stare, my dick hardening inside my own Speedo. I knew then that I had to have you, at some point in my life, I had to have you. I wanted to stick my head inside that beautiful ass, run my tongue down its crack and underneath to the balls, suck on your cock while pinching those amazing nipples, feeling the rounded pecs, staring up as you flexed your massive arms. You took the sunglasses off for a moment, looked across the pool, and our eyes locked. You gave me a small smile, nodded your head, acknowledging me, and sat back down.

You noticed me.

I know you did.

You acknowledged my interest.

I spent the rest of that afternoon watching you, trying to steel my nerve to go over and talk to you. You had nodded at me, after all, I knew you were interested, but it was such a bright day, and everyone around the pool would notice me walking over there, even if it was just in their peripheral vision, and see me sit down, and what if, by some weird chance that was barely comprehensible to me, you weren't actually interested? There was that, and my own fear that if I even got close to you, my dick would get so hard everyone could see it, and in my white Speedo it would be pretty obvious, and there was the very strong chance that I would crawl up between your legs and suck your dick right there. Somehow I didn't think you were the exhibitionist type—yeah, sure, you liked to show off your body in that little piece of yellow Lycra, but somehow I didn't think you were the type who liked to have his cock sucked in a public place.

Finally around four you put your shorts on and left. You turned at the door and looked back at me. My dick was so hard it hurt. My balls ached. I should have gone after you, but I didn't. That was stupid. I've regretted it ever since.

When I got home I had to beat off. I lay down on my bed and covered my aching dick with lube. I closed my eyes and started stroking, remembering every move you made, every inch of your body, the way your muscles moved, the way your pecs moved when you laughed the way your ass moved when you walked, everything. I shot a big load for you, man in a Speedo, a big load that even hit me in the face...I had never shot a load that hard before jacking off. I've shot them before when I was with a guy that really turned me on, but never ever when I was jacking off. It was you. I knew then you were my fate, my destiny.

We were meant to be together.

You probably don't even remember the first time I ever sucked your cock, do you? It was the next weekend, at the bathhouse. I don't even remember why I went there. Probably the reason I always went there—no-frills, no-strings sex, sex without having to make conversation, to go through the usual bar mating rituals...they are kind of tiresome, don't you think? That's probably why you were there in the bathhouse yourself. You must get so tired of going into bars and having every man in there hitting on you, touching you, coming on to you. I don't blame you for being there...you didn't know when we were going to run into each other again. I didn't know if I would ever see you again myself. I was almost beginning to think you were something I imagined. Surely there wasn't such a perfect man out there running around. I had almost convinced myself when I saw you at the bathhouse with that towel tied around your waist. I couldn't believe my eyes. The towel didn't reveal as much skin as the Speedo, of course, but I was able to see plenty when you walked past me up the stairs to the area with all the glory holes. I followed you up the stairs, watching your massive calves flex and move. You went into a booth. The one next to it was open and I ducked into it, latching it behind me. I went over to the glory hole looking into your booth. I got down on my knees. I looked through. I couldn't see your face, but I could see the towel sitting on a chair. I could see your ass, your beautiful white ass, outlined in a Speedo tan line. You turned and walked over to the glory hole and stuck your big, thick, hard dick through it. I put my mouth on it and started sucking. My dick was hard so I started pulling on it. I wished I could reach up and touch your pecs, feel your legs. It was pure torture being there on the other side of the wall, only able to put my mouth on that beautiful cock. I worshipped your cock, licking it, sucking it, nibbling on it just a little, hoping you would bless me by coming in my face. I couldn't hold it back any longer, shooting my own load while working on yours, but then you pulled back away. I could see you wrapping the towel around you again and then you were gone. I tried to go after you, see if you wanted to come back to my room, but I never saw you again that night, and I scoured the bathhouse. I finally went home about five in the morning.

I knew I would see you again.

You were my destiny.

We belong together.

Imagine my delight when you came into the bank that following Monday morning. When I saw you standing there in line, wearing your suit, looking so damned handsome, I almost shot a load into my pants. The other tellers noticed you, too, I saw them darting glances at you. I knew that you would wind up at my window. I just knew it. It was destiny. And sure enough, you came to me, giving me your deposit slip and your paycheck. Somehow, it wasn't appropriate then for me to say anything to you. I couldn't very well say, "Hey, I sucked your dick last Saturday night, give me a call sometime, okay?" No, I couldn't do that. But the nice thing was your deposit slip gave me your name. Jason Westfall. Your phone number and your address, too. After you left, I copied all the information down on my notepad.

I drove past your house that night. I was impressed. A really nice Victorian double on Constance Street. A wooden fence around the backyard. Roses in the front yard. All restored and pretty. It was so much nicer than my roach trap apartment in the Bywater. I drove around the block and passed by it again. Yes, it looked like it would make a really nice home for the two of us. I parked for a moment across the street, watching the house, stroking my hard dick through my pants. That's when the inspiration hit me. I went back to my apartment and beat off into a pair of black underwear, the same underwear I wore that night to the bathhouse. It seemed like the right thing to do. I knew you needed a sign from me that I knew about our attraction, about our destiny. So, I boxed up the underwear with my come in it and mailed it to you.

I only wish I had been there the day it arrived. Did you open it and know what it was? Did you rub it over your pecs, your stomach, your balls, your legs, your ass? Did you hold it up to your nose to get my smell, did you know my come was dried on it? Did you try to suck my come out?

I do love you so very very much.

Every day, I wondered if you were looking for me, too. I wondered every morning when I went to work if that would be the day when you would come in to my window, and slip me the note saying that you loved the gift I had sent you, but you would rather have the real thing. Every time my phone rang, I wondered if it was you, if you had managed to unearth my phone number and were calling to invite me over. I wanted to call you, so many times I picked up the phone and started dialing, but stopped. I knew the next move in our little game of seduction had to come from you, and I couldn't make it easy for you. No, that would be wrong. I needed you to show me you cared. I needed to see you making an effort too, darling man in a Speedo. It couldn't all just be from me. There were so many nights that I wondered if I was making it too hard. Maybe you just weren't as smart as me. Okay, it was just plain luck—no, make that destiny—that brought you into the bank to me. So maybe you needed just a little help.

That's when I took the pictures of my cock and mailed them to you. You liked getting the pictures, didn't you? It made you hard, didn't it? You jacked off, pinching your nipples, looking at them, didn't you? Every time I was beating off I was thinking about you. I couldn't stop thinking about you. I dreamed about you, about you fucking me in that pretty little house on Constance Street, just bending me over the kitchen table and ramming that beautiful thick cock into my ass, fucking me senseless, pounding into me so damned hard that the table sometimes moved, that sometimes I was lifted off my feet by the intensity of your need to plunge so deeply into me. I dreamed about you trapping me down on the bed, holding my arms in your powerful hands over my head, shoving your cock into my face, slapping me with its hardness, rubbing it on my face, my eyes, my lips, blowing a load into my hair. I dreamed about showering with you, running a bar of soap over your slick wet body, lathering up your armpits, your chest, your ass, your balls. I was driving past your house every night now, going to the country club every Sunday hoping to see you, going to the bathhouse every Saturday night thinking you might be there, looking for me…

But you never were.

Why did you tease me like that?

You knew how badly I wanted you.

You knew how badly I wanted to be your toy, your slave, your pig.

That guy you were seeing? He was all wrong for you, man in a Speedo. What did you see in him? Yeah, sure, he was pretty and had a nice body and all that, but he was just wrong. You two didn't fit together. I couldn't believe it when I saw you letting him into your house, kissing him so passionately. Oh, I didn't expect you to be celibate while you were waiting to find me, I know you had needs and all that, but that guy? Sure he was young and pretty and muscular, but he was all wrong for you. I stayed there, sitting in my car, parked down the street, for several hours waiting for him to leave. I followed him home—he lived in the Marigny. I parked and went and knocked on his door shortly after he went in. He came to the door and said, "yes?" I told him he was all wrong for you, that you loved me and no one else, and I would greatly appreciate it if he would stay away from you in the future, and then he started yelling at me, telling me it was none of my business and who the hell was I anyway? I grabbed him so he would stop yelling, grabbed him by the throat and pushed him back inside his house, and I told him who I was, your true love, your destiny, and he was just a little whore, nothing more, you couldn't possibly love him, we were meant to be together and he just had to understand that, and I kept hold of his throat and he tried to pull my hands off, and I wouldn't let go, I had to make him understand.

I didn't mean to kill him.

I killed for you, man in a Speedo.

Do you see how much I love you?

That's why, you see, I finally had to just come over here and see you. It just wasn't going fast enough for me. I know, I know, I should be more patient, should have just let things develop the way fate intended, but it hurt me, it really hurt me, to see you with that little whore. It hurt, man in a Speedo, and I don't know if I could go through that kind of pain again.

Are the ropes too tight? I'm sorry. But don't you see I had to tie you up? So you would listen to me? So I could explain it all to you? I love you. I love you. I know the gag isn't comfortable…but I couldn't be interrupted until I was finished pouring my heart out to you. Besides, you look so beautiful all stretched out there, naked. You can't hide that hard-on from me, man in a Speedo. You like being tied up, don't you? You know I would never hurt you. I love you too much to hurt you.

Your pecs feel wonderful, they really do.

I kind of like the way you tremble every time I touch you.

You like it too, don't you?

You want me to suck your dick, don't you?

Of course I am going to let you go, man in a Speedo. But first, I am going to have this night with you.

After that, you can decide for yourself what you want.

I know it will be me.

It has to be.

You understand, don't you?

## WROUGHT IRON LACE

The guy who just moved in across the courtyard is gorgeous.

I would guess that he's still in his early thirties, maybe still the late twenties. Since I turned forty it's really hard for me to judge age. Twenty-year-olds look like babies, fifty-year-olds look forty, and that group in between I just have no fucking clue. I watched him move in the day after I came home from the hospital. I have three pins in my leg from the car accident, and I have to keep it elevated as much as possible. I can't stand on it yet, even with crutches, so I have a nice loaner wheelchair from the hospital. Friends are running errands for me when they can, and checking in on me to make sure I'm not lying on the floor in the bathroom helpless. I don't think I've ever spent so much time at home by myself. It's amazing how little there is to watch on television, even with eighty cable channels. Is there anyone left on the planet who has *not* yet seen the movie *Sixteen Candles*? Why do they have to keep airing it?

It was a Saturday, and if ever there was a day of television hell, it's Saturday. There's nothing on, at any time of the day. I don't really care that much about billiards, snowboarding, or timber sport, thank you very much. I knew the vacant apartment on the other side of the courtyard had been rented, the lower one, but I'd forgotten someone was moving in. My apartment is the second floor of a converted slave quarter, and my balcony has a view straight into the living room and bedroom windows of the lower in the back of the main house. I had seen the young lesbian couple who had lived there naked in the bedroom entirely too many times, and had trained myself not to notice those windows.

What can I say? I was bored, bored, bored. It was eleven o'clock in the morning, I'd been up for three hours, and I wasn't expecting anyone to come by again until two o'clock. I put a Jewel CD on and pushed myself out onto the balcony. It was a beautiful October morning, the sky blue, the sun shining and warm, but none of the humidity that made New Orleans almost unlivable in the summer. There was a stack of books on the balcony table, and I figured this enforced captivity was a pretty good time to catch up on my reading. On top of the stack was a hardcover with two incredibly pretty young men giving each other the eye on the jacket. They were fully dressed, so I knew it was a romance rather than some porn. The sex would be soft-core, the characters fairly two-dimensional, and the problems they faced would be most likely vapid, but it would while away some time without requiring a vast degree of thought.

The door in the gate opened, and this guy came in. Wow, was my instant reaction. I put the book down on the table. He was wearing a black tank tee, tight black jean shorts that reached almost to his knees, with the bottom inch or so rolled up, and calfskin ankle boots with heavy socks pushed down on top of them. He was wearing a black baseball cap with the fleur-de-lis emblem of the Saints on the front. He had a key ring in his hand, and he walked right over to the door of the vacant apartment and unlocked it. When his back turned to me, my jaw dropped. He had without a doubt the most beautiful ass I have ever seen in my entire life. It was hard, it was round, perfectly curved. It was an ass to make men weep, an ass that belonged on an underwear box, an ass that could launch a thousand hard-ons.

I lit a cigarette.

A couple of other guys, muscular, attractive enough but nothing like the first, came into the back carrying boxes. Any other time, I would have probably been attracted to either or both of them, but the incredible beauty of the first boy (I found myself thinking of him as a "boy," strangely) made them seem like the girls who don't make the Top Ten at Miss America. I'm sure they were used to it—it probably happened to them in bars all the time. I sat there for several hours, watching them move boxes and furniture, occasionally breaking to have a beer or a smoke break at one of the iron tables in the courtyard. The also-rans eventually removed their shirts, displaying fairly nice torsos, one with some hair, the other completely smooth. Again, under ordinary circumstances I would have been fantasizing a pretty damned vivid three-way scene. If I could walk I'd be down there helping, flirting a little, feeling them out about trysting. I would watch the sweat glistening on their bare skin in the sun and wonder how it might taste, if their armpits were becoming a little smelly perhaps from the sweat, if their underwear was sticking to their asses. But my mind was solely on my new neighbor, hoping that he too would take his shirt off, give me a glimpse of his chest and back, maybe the waistband of his underwear showing above his shorts. It never occurred to me that they might be aware of me, the aging man in the wheelchair up on the balcony watching them hungrily without even saying hello. I never saw them look up or give any indication they were being watched. For all I knew, when they were out of sight on the street taking stuff out of the truck they could be laughing their ass off at the perv on the balcony, thinking he's hidden behind the wrought iron lacework. But if that were the case, it wouldn't have mattered to me at all. I could not tear myself away from watching the boy in the black tank tee.

They did talk loud enough for me to finally figure out their names: my neighbor was Mike, the tall redhead was appropriately enough Sandy, and the shorter Italian-looking guy's name was Axel. They were easy with each other, joking and teasing in that way people who have been friends for a long time have. Every once in a while one of them would say something as incomprehensible to me as Sanskrit, and they would all burst into hysterical laughter. They each knew the secret language of their friendship, which had been learned over too many drinks at the bar on Saturday night, from brunch on Sundays, from long, involved phone conversations. The rest of us were excluded from it.

I found myself wondering if Mike was dating either one of them, if there was more than friendship between them.

I also wondered if Mike slept with his curtains closed.

I watched until they apparently were finished, Mike's shirt remaining on the entire time, as though he were teasing me, knowing how desperate I was to see his bare torso. His shirt was wet with sweat, and it clung to him tantalizingly, just enough for me to see the outline of his round pecs, his flat stomach, to see the play of the muscles in his back. It was around four when Sandy and Axel took off, left Mike to deal with the boxes and the bags and the assorted debris of his life. I sat there on my balcony, watching the bedroom window, and sure enough, after a few moments Mike walked in carrying a can of Diet Pepsi. He stood in front of the dresser, reached down, and started pulling the shirt over his head. His skin was tanned, firm, supple and smooth as silk. He wiped his face with the shirt before tossing it into a laundry basket, and took a big drink from the can. The muscles in his arms moved under his skin, the afternoon sun glinting on the sweat. He moved out of sight. I sat there for another few minutes, hoping that he would come back, remove the shorts and underwear, but the seconds ticked away maddeningly.

Reluctantly, I pushed myself back into the apartment.

I spent the rest of the day avoiding the balcony. Some friends came by to bring me dinner and cigarettes, I must have flipped through the channels about a thousand times per hour, and finally around ten I gave up and went to bed.

I woke up at three in the morning. Wide awake, staring at the ceiling, unable to go back to sleep. I lifted myself into the annoying wheelchair and pushed myself out into the living room. I lit a cigarette, but resisted turning on the lights. I wheeled myself out onto the balcony. The night was quiet, even though the insanity of Bourbon Street was just a block away. I sat there, staring at the clouds reflecting the neon of the Quarter back down at us, and was about to light another cigarette when I heard the gate to the courtyard slam shut. I heard laughter.

Sure enough, it was Mike and some guy. Mike's shirt was tucked into the back of his jeans, his torso glistening with sweat in the moonlight as he tried to put his key in the lock. I couldn't get a look at the face of the guy he was with, but it wasn't either Axel or Sandy. The moon just then came out from behind a cloud, and as the silvery light bathed the courtyard in an eerie almost otherworldly glow, I got a good look at Mike's companion.

I knew the guy—his name was Blake something or another. I'd seen him around in the bars for years, dancing with his shirt off. He was very big. He towered over Mike as he stood back waiting for Mike to get the door open. He was about six-three and weighed about two hundred and thirty pounds of thick muscle. His pecs were as big as cantaloupes. His biceps were bigger than my head. His ass was big and thick and meaty. I had many times watched him moving on the dance floor with his shirt off, hoping against hope to catch his eye. It never happened. Well, I never really expected it to, you know? Great big muscle boys never noticed guys like me. No, they only noticed other muscle boys or hot little numbers like Mike.

The door finally opened and they went inside. The living room light shone through the blinds. I went ahead and lit the cigarette.

The bedroom light came on.

The two of them entered, and I caught my breath. Blake was carrying him. Mike had his legs wrapped around Blake's waist, his arms wrapped around his head, and they were kissing. Blake's hands were firmly planted on Mike's ass. He turned and set Mike down on the dresser and stepped back. Mike's hands went to Blake's belt buckle, unfastening it and tearing the buttons open on the fly of Blake's jeans. The jeans slipped down a bit, and I could see the top of Blake's ass. It was white against his dark tan, wiry black hairs running in a patch just above the whiteness where the deep crevice between the thick cheeks began.

Mike grinned at him and yanked Blake's pants down.

Oh, man.

Mike slid down off the dresser to his knees, slightly pressuring Blake to turn a bit to the side. By doing so, I could see Blake's long thick cock, his low-hanging purplish balls, the thatch of black hair. Mike's tongue flicked out, licking the head of it, and Blake brought both of his hands down on top of Mike's head. Blake tilted his own head back, his eyes closed, as Mike started working on his cock, slicking it with his spit, his mouth moving back and forth, his hands moving up to tweak Blake's big round nipples, then squeezing those massive pecs, pinching and pulling on the nipples again.

I dropped my hand to my own dick, which was erect.

Blake reached down and put his hands underneath Mike's armpits, and the muscles in his upper body flexed as he lifted Mike bodily into the air. He set Mike down on the dresser again, opening Mike's shorts and yanking them off. His tongue snaked out and he began licking Mike's neck, then moving down the center of his chest. Mike's head went back, his eyes closed, and Blake pulled Mike's white boxer briefs down. Mike's dick was smaller than Blake's, but thick, nestled in perfectly trimmed hair. Blake's head went down and I knew he was sucking on Mike.

This was better than any porn tape I owned.

Blake raised his head from Mike's dick, which glistened with spit. He reached under Mike's arms again and picked him up, turning him so that he was standing on the dresser with that beautiful ass right in front of Blake's face. He pushed Mike's thighs apart, reached up and spread the firm white cheeks, and then his face went in. Mike's back arched, rounding his ass even more as Blake feasted upon his asshole. Mike's arms and back flexed as he shifted slightly, writhing from the pleasure of Blake's tongue licking and probing him. Blake's hands smacked the white roundness, leaving reddish prints, over and over again.

I could almost hear the sound of hand striking flesh.

Blake stood back for a moment, and Mike turned to face him, squatting down until he was sitting on the dresser. His eyes were half-closed, his hair slick with sweat. Blake grabbed hold of his ankles and pushed them up in the air, until Mike was lying on his back, his ass hanging off the end, his legs up in the air.

Blake shoved his cock into Mike's ass.

Mike's back arched up, his abdominal muscles springing out, his mouth open, his head going back.

I could almost hear the moan coming from between his lips, the moan of pleasure, as Blake slowly slid back. Mike's body trembled as Blake paused, then flexed his meaty ass and shoved all the way back in. Again, Mike's body convulsed.

My cock started to leak a little.

The strokes I made on my own dick were slow and steady, matching Blake's inside Mike's ass.

I wished I had a video camera. Watching them was better than the best porn I owned.

Blake brought his big hands down on Mike's chest, squeezing, kneading, pinching. Mike's face was lost in the joy of getting so thoroughly fucked, fucked by a beautiful big muscle stud who knew how to fuck a pretty boy.

Mike's calves were resting on Blake's big shoulders.

The rhythm of the fucking began to pick up.

Blake must be getting close, I realized, increasing the stroke speed of my own hand.

Mike's entire body tensed up as Blake sped up, the strokes still long and deep, just faster and faster.

Come began spraying out of Mike's cock, shooting up and splashing on his stomach, chest. One shot flew over his head.

Blake pulled his cock out and shot his big load all over Mike's torso.

They stood still for a moment, frozen in a moment of time.

Blake leaned down and they kissed.

And I came, my load shooting up into the air, all over my hand and arm.

They moved out of my line of sight.

I lit another cigarette, my breath coming in gasps.

I wiped my arm and hand off with a towel.

I sat there, smoking, for a moment, replaying the scene again in my head. My dick began to stir again.

Mike's front door opened, and they walked out. Blake had his jeans on again, his shirt tucked into the back. Mike was wearing his white boxer briefs. They glowed a bit in the moonlight. They walked together to the gate, around the corner of the main house, out of my sight. I heard the gate open and close.

Mike walked back into the courtyard and over to his front door. He paused for a moment on the sill, then turned and looked right up at me.

He raised his right hand and waved, a smile on his face.

The door shut behind him.

And I wondered, in the darkness behind my wrought iron lace, when the next show would be.

## THE PORN KING AND I

H e is beautiful.
    He is everything I want in a lover.
  Thick curly black hair.
  Blue eyes.
  Muscles rippling under tan skin.
  A hard, round, beautiful ass.
  The cock of a Greek god.
  I first saw him in a poster in the adult book store on Decatur Street. The poster was black with just a picture of him, hands on hips, wearing a jock strap. His face was smiling, a warm, inviting smile that would melt anyone's heart and stir their groin. His tanned skin gleamed. At the bottom of the poster in red capital letters it said: CODY DALLAS IN THE SEX SENSE. I stood, staring for a few moments, my glance going from that pretty face down the neck to the beautifully shaped chest, smooth and silky, down the abs that looked carved out of stone, to the top of the jock. His hard-on was unmistakable beneath the white cloth. I walked over to the counter. "Do you have that film?" I pointed back over my shoulder with my thumb.

  The counter boy was just that; a boy. He didn't look old enough to be working in a sex shop. Hell, he didn't look old enough to have hair on his balls. Bleached blond hair standing up spikily over black roots. A straggle of hair on his chin that was supposed to be a goatee. He weighed maybe 130 pounds. His baggy jeans hung off his hips. A black Marilyn Manson T-shirt. Pierced nose and eyebrow. Tattoos on both arms. He grinned at me. Braces.

"Yeah. Only $59.95, or did you want to rent?"

"I'll buy."

I walked home to my apartment on Chartres Street. Opened the door. Switched on the television with the remote. Opened the box and popped the video in. Hit Play as I pulled off my shirt, kicked off my shoes, stripped naked. Reached underneath the couch for the fresh bottle of poppers and the lube. Fast-forward through the opening credits. First scene.

It's him. He is wearing Daisy Dukes and work boots. No shirt. The sun glistens on the muscles in his back. He is trimming a bush with garden clippers. Every movement he makes causes muscles to ripple. Someone is watching from the house. Behind the curtains a face appears. Cut away to from behind the curtains. He looks beautiful, oh so beautiful. Camera pulls back. The man at the window is naked. Thinner. Not as muscled as Cody. Lean wiry muscle.

Cody looks up at the window and smiles. The man in the window beckons. Cody puts the clippers down and walks to the door. It opens.

I open the bottle of poppers. My eyes are glued to the screen. I lift it up to my right nostril. I close off the left and inhale. Deeply. The scent fills my nose, my sinuses, my lungs. I shift it to the other nostril. Inhale.

My cock starts to stir as they kiss. Tongue. Arms going around each other. Cody grabs the man's ass with both hands and pulls him closer. Crotches grinding. The blond man has a hard-on. He is massaging Cody's ass. The poppers start to hit. My cock springs to attention. I play with my right nipple, pulling on it, pinching it. It feels good. Cody moves down and starts tonguing the guy's nipple.

"Oh yeah," I say.

The blond moans.

Cody moves down. His tongue shoots out and licks the tip of the blond's cock. It's a big one. It's pink. He starts licking it. Cut to the blond's face. Eyes closed. Moaning. Yeah baby, suck that dick, suck it good.

I take another whiff.

The blond's big dick disappears. Cody is working it good. My balls ache. I want to touch my cock but don't. The blond keeps moaning. Yeah yeah suck it man, that's it, that's the way.

I can feel Cody's warm mouth on mine.

His tongue is velvety.

"Yeah," I say. "Suck that cock right."

Cody is undoing his shorts. The camera angle shifts to behind him. The blond is hairless and pale. Cody straightens up and the shorts drop. His bare ass is round, hard, firm. There is a thin white line that runs above each cheek and meets in a tiny triangle above his crack.

It is beautiful.

"Oh, man."

I take another whiff.

My blood is pounding. I can hear my heartbeat as Cody stands up and turns around. His pubic hair is trimmed. His balls hang, round, heavy. His thick, swollen cock juts out. The blond sinks to his knees behind him. The camera moves to around behind the blond, who buries his face inside Cody's ass.

Close-up.

His tongue darts into the hole.

Cody moans. Eat my ass, baby, yeah eat that ass right.

I can taste him. I can feel that hard ass on either side of my face. The blond reaches up and slaps a cheek. Hard. The crack of the slap is like a whip. Cody moans again. A red handprint appears on his left ass cheek.

My hand tingles.

"Come on," I say. I can taste his ass. I run my tongue over my lips. He tastes so good, so clean.

Cody slips on a condom.

The blond turns around and bends over.

"Yeah, fuck me, Cody."

I lie back on the couch. My legs go up in the air and apart. My cock is aching, begging me to touch it. I take another whiff. My body starts to tremble.

He enters.

The blond's eyes close and he moans again. Fuck me with that cock, yeah, man, make me scream.

I can feel it, the swollen head forcing its way into my hole. My teeth start to chatter.

I reach for the lube and slowly pour a thin stream onto my cock.

Cody smacks the blond's ass.

I jump.

"Fuck me Cody, yeah fuck me, make me your bitch."

He's all the way in.

It feels incredible. He is filling me up, moving so slow that my breath comes in gasps. He is teasing me, teasing me with his cock, because he knows that I want it fast and deep and hard. I want him to tear me in half. I spread the lube with my fingers until my whole cock is wet.

The blond is moaning louder.

My moans rise to match his.

The camera cuts to behind. Cody's hard ass is flexing and

thrusting. It is beautiful. I stick my tongue out and taste him again, taste that sweet hole. I can smell its musty odor. I lift the poppers to my nose again.

Just breathe.

A side angle now. The blond is turning over and lying down on his back on the bed. Without missing a beat Cody slams into him again. His abs flex. The blond pulls on his dick. The blond's body reverberates with each thrust.

I touch my cock. My whole body is trembling with need, the need to release my come, to let it go and spray.

The feel of his cock in me is like nothing I've ever felt before.

"Fuck me Cody fuck me hard, come on."

My hand moves faster.

The blond is alternating between cries and whimpers.

Cody keeps pounding away.

I feel it rising, the come boiling in my balls. My cock gets harder. I can feel it rising, moving up into my cock.

The blond screams, come showering over his chest.

Cody pulls back, stroking his cock.

It explodes out of me. My breath comes in stitches. I am panting, my body trembling as my cock fires shot after shot onto my chest, my stomach, my neck, my face.

My body shakes as I suck in air.

Cody moans as ropy strings of come squirt out of him, onto the blond's chest and stomach.

I stare as Cody bends down to kiss him and rub their commingled juices into the blond's skin.

I reach for a towel.

I wipe down my cock, which is still semi-hard.

I press Stop on the remote control.

I wipe off my torso and my face.

I pick up the video box and kiss Cody's face.

So beautiful.

"I love you," I whisper.

I turn off the television and lie back down on the couch naked. I can feel his arms around me as I drift off to sleep.

"I love you," he whispers back in my ear. "I love you."

I love you.

## Will You Love Me in September?

W ill you love me in September?"
Kevin's voice, his words, echo in Tom's head even after he hangs up the telephone, placing the receiver back into its cradle. He gets out of the bed slowly, gently, not jarring the mattress, and walks over to the patio windows, turning the cord that opens the blinds so that the sunlight spills into the room. The heat of a summer morning in Tampa comes in with the sunlight, and he turns and looks back at the bed, where he can see the smooth outline of—

Sean? Scott? Steve? Sean, that's it, isn't it? Did it really matter?—sleeping, snoring softly, and he feels it then, what he knew he would feel last night in the bar when Sean? Scott? Steve? came over and started talking to him, flirting with him, knowing full well that he should not be responding, but he was nice-looking, had a nice body, and he was so obviously interested, and he felt the interest stirring in his groin, and he knew if Sean? Scott? Steve? wanted him, he would bring him home.

"Will you love me in September?"

It had been so long since he had seen Kevin, almost a month, that month stretching into eternity, a bottomless abyss that cannot be conquered, and the phone calls, each one at least an hour in duration, making him think that he should buy stock in AT&T and maybe that way he could get some of the money back they were spending on long distance, the phone calls were nice and made Tom feel warm and reassured and loved, but he could not curl up with the phone in bed at night, he could not get a hug from the phone after a particularly bad day, Kevin was two thousand miles away in Cleveland, the phone calls were just not enough. But I do love him, he thinks again, looking at Sean? Scott? Steve?'s form and feeling like a whore, feeling unworthy of Kevin's love, undeserving of anyone's devotion.

"Will you love me in September?"

And Sean? Scott? Steve? began to make the unmistakable signs of interest, the gay mating ritual, the occasional touches, brushing up against him, and he knew that Sean? Scott? Steve? wanted him, it wasn't just his imagination, he was being cruised and he was being cruised hard, it was not going to be a relationship, it was just a one-night stand, it had nothing to do with Kevin, or how he felt about Kevin, it was just a fucking one-night stand and he didn't have to tell Kevin about it. Kevin didn't have to know, he was two thousand miles away, Kevin knew no one in Orlando except for him, so how would Kevin ever know? Only if I tell him, he thought, and he wanted Sean? Scott? Steve?, he wanted to be kissed and hugged and held, and loved, even if love had nothing to do with it. It was just a one-night stand. It meant nothing.

"Will you love me in September?"

And it wasn't like it was the first time. But was it really cheating? After all, even though he loved Kevin and Kevin loved him, there was the distance thing, and there was no guarantee they would ever be together. Moving in together would be great but that was still months away, and Kevin wouldn't be coming to see him until September, flying in for only four days, four wonderful days that they were going to be together, introducing Kevin to all his friends, showing Kevin his life and what it was like, what he was going to be giving up to move to Orlando to be with the first man he had fallen in love with in over ten years, an emotion he had begun to think he was no longer capable of feeling. He looks over at Sean? Scott? Steve? and wonders again if he was capable of ever truly loving anyone.

"Will you love me in September?"

He walks out of the bedroom into the kitchen and starts a pot of coffee. He pours cereal into a bowl, fat free of course, and adds 1 percent milk, after all, can't take a chance with the body, can't take a chance with the body, can't ever take the chance that the weight will come back, it took far too long to take it off and turn some of it into the muscle that now got him noticed in the clubs and bars. He would be giving that up too, to be with Kevin, the attention that he now got in clubs when he went out, the admiring looks, the lustful glances that led to people like Sean or Steve or Scott or whatever his name was in his bed, the sweaty impassioned embraces, the moans, the no strings attached. After all of those years of being a bar wallflower, not being noticed, only being ignored, it was so nice to walk into a bar and see someone hot looking him up and down, trying (and sometimes succeeding) to make eye contact…can he give that up?

"Will you love me in September?"

The coffee finally ready, he fills a cup and adds a packet of Sweet'n Low and a splash of fat free International Delight French vanilla creamer to the max, and can hear Sean? Scott? Steve? stirring in the bedroom. He sits down at the table, staring across at the blinds that shield the living room from that intense Florida sun, wondering, wondering, wondering. Do I love Kevin? Does Kevin really love me? The phone calls, once so sweet and loving and touching, are beginning to get a little bit on the scary side to him. But is it fear of commitment? Fear of love? A feeling that perhaps he doesn't deserve to be loved? A self-destructive urge? Is that what led him to bring home Sean? Scott? Steve? last night, wrap himself into unheard of ecstasies, and pleasures, smothering him with kisses, yet all the while thinking to himself that he wished Sean? Scott? Steve? was actually Kevin, that it was Kevin he was kissing and making love to, Kevin's body entwined with his while he slept, Kevin, Kevin, Kevin...

"Will you love me in September?"

Sean? Scott? Steve? walks into the living room, wearing only a pair of black Calvin Kleins, his hair standing up, scratching the side of his head, yawning. His smoothly muscled body ripples as he walks, and he looks at him, remembering suddenly what had attracted him to this beautiful boy in the first place, and despite everything that has been racing through his head since talking to Kevin on the telephone earlier, he feels that familiar longing. Morning, baby, he says, and Sean? Scott? Steve? smiles, showing perfect teeth, his blue eyes flashing with—with happiness? Could that be what it was? he asked himself, but there is no question, whatever it is, Sean? Scott? Steve? is very pretty. Do you want some coffee? Sean? Steve? Scott? nods, and he goes into the kitchen, gets a cup out of the cupboard that says *HOTLANTA* on it, and as he is filling it with coffee Sean? Scott? Steve comes up behind him, slipping his arms around him, and kisses him on the neck. Morning, beautiful, he says, nuzzles his neck. He almost spills the coffee on the stark white counter. Beautiful? He thinks I am beautiful.

"Will you love me in September?"

Kevin thinks he is beautiful, too. It is such a weird feeling, a weird thought, to be considered beautiful. After being the

Ugly Duckling for so long, to be considered beautiful, after dieting and joining a gym and religiously working out three times a week, that was all it took, and now the compliments and attention come, there isn't a night when he can't go out to a club and get laid if he so chooses, and not just a desperation lay either, but a fairly hot-looking guy, the days of "settling" are over, despite the fact that he hates to be superficial, he hates what he is slowly turning into, someone who bases everything on looks and appearance, the very people he used to hate on those few occasions when he mustered up the nerve to go out to the clubs, because they wouldn't look at him or even try to give him a chance, wanting to scream at them I'm a good person! I'm funny! I'm clever! I'm fun! but they didn't care, because all that mattered was the way he looked, and now he is turning into one of them, and how many truly nice and wonderful people is he allowing the opportunity to get to know slip by because he is out trolling for hot studs? But now the Ugly Duckling is a swan, and his Prince has finally come, even though he lives two thousand miles away, and he loves Kevin, he truly does, and people like Sean? Scott? Steve? mean nothing to him but a roll in the hay and sexual release, but would Kevin understand that? Would Kevin forgive that? He doesn't think so. Cream and sugar? he asks as Sean? Scott? Steve? continues to nuzzle on his neck, trying to ignore the goose bumps rising on his arms, trying to ignore the rush of blood to his crotch, the growing lust.

"Will you love me in September?"

And so he turns, and their lips meet, he has to reach up and go up on the balls of his feet to reach Sean? Scott? Steve? He didn't remember him as being quite that tall, but his lips are soft yet firm, and his own part, and the tongue passes between them, gently probing, and he closes his lips around it and sucks on it softly, gently, tenderly, delicately. Sean?

Scott? Steve? moans a little, and he lets his hands reach down, encircling his hard buttocks, and their bodies press tightly together, and he runs his hands over Sean? Scott? Steve?'s firm hairless back, and then their lips part, and he smiles up at his lover, no, don't call him that, Kevin is his lover, not this pretty blond boy that he has no business being with, and then Sean? Scott? Steve? is saying, let's shower, do you have a toothbrush I can borrow, and he is answering yes, of course, I buy them in bulk at Sam's, and he thinks how that sounds, like he buys toothbrushes in bulk because he has so many one-night stands he needs a cheap and regular supply, but he really buys them because he changes toothbrushes every week, it was anal retentive, he knew, but it was something that his mother always insisted on when he was growing up, and it was something he still sticks to, even now, now that he's in his thirties, mother of God, how old is Sean? Scott? Steve? he can't be much older than twenty-five, can he? and then for curiosity's sake he asks, and Sean? Scott? Steve? asks if it matters, and then adds twenty-seven, and he answers I would have thought twenty-two or three and he is told thank you, and kissed again for his flattery, although it wasn't really flattery, it was an honest opinion.

"Will you love me in September?"

The shower is running, the water is so hot, there is steam rising out of it and the mirrors have already begun to fog over, and he follows him into the stream of water, and they are lathering each other slowly, gently, carefully, and it is erotic, he can feel himself getting excited again, wet flesh touching wet flesh, stroking and slipping and sliding and giggling and moaning and kissing and touching and—

"Will you love me in September?"

And he is dressed and gone, and the apartment is silent, quiet, and he can still hear Kevin's voice, asking those words over and over again like a litany, as though he is running his fingers over rosary beads as he recites the words, and Kevin loves him, he knows he loves him, he loves him so very much, and he doesn't deserve it anymore, he has cheated, he cannot be faithful, he is unworthy of Kevin's love, and the best thing for him to do is to set Kevin free, Kevin deserves to be free from this horrible long distance love affair that is only destined to bring pain, and he doesn't want to hurt Kevin, he loves Kevin, and so he heads over to the telephone and dials Kevin's number and Kevin answers, and he hears that voice, and the excitement in it when Kevin recognizes his voice, he realizes that he can't do it.

"I will love you in September," he says softly into the telephone, hating himself for the words, even though they are true.

"I will love you in September."

## BLOODLETTING

The damp air was thick with the scent of blood.

It had been days since I had last fed, and the desire was gnawing at my insides. I stood up, and my eyes focused on a young man walking a bicycle in front of the cathedral. He was talking on a cell phone, his face animated and agitated. He was wearing a T-shirt that read *Who Dat Say They Gonna Beat Dem Saints?* and a pair of ratty old paint-spattered jeans cut off at the knees. There was a tattoo of Tweety Bird on his right calf, and another indistinguishable one on his left forearm. His hair was dark, combed to a peak in the center of his head, and his face was flushed. He stopped walking, his voice getting louder and louder as his face got darker.

I could smell his blood. I could almost hear his beating heart.

I could see the pulsing vein in his neck, beckoning me forward.

The sun was setting, and the lights around Jackson Square were starting to come on. The tarot card readers were folding up their tables, ready to disappear into the night. The band playing in front of the cathedral was putting their instruments away. The artists who hung their work on the iron fence around the park were long gone, as were the living statues. The square, so teeming with life just a short hour earlier, was emptying of people, and the setting sun was taking the warmth with it as it slowly disappeared in the west. The cold breeze coming from the river ruffled my hair a bit as I watched the young man with the bicycle. He started wheeling the bicycle forward again, still talking on the phone. He reached the concrete ramp leading up to Chartres Street. He stopped just as he reached the street, and I focused my hearing as he became more agitated. *What do you want me to say? You're just being a bitch, and anything I say you're just going to turn around on me.*

I felt the burning inside.

Desire was turning into need.

I knew it was best to satisfy the desire before it became need. I could feel the knots of pain from deprivation forming behind each of my temples and knew it was almost too late. I shouldn't have let it go this long, but I wanted to test my limits, see how long I could put off the hunger. I'd been taught to feed daily, which would keep the hunger under control and keep me out of danger.

Need was dangerous. Need led a vampire to take risks he wouldn't take ordinarily. And risks could lead to exposure, to a painful death.

The first lesson I'd learned was to always satiate the hunger while it was still desire, to never *ever* let it become need.

I had waited too long.

He started walking again, and I began following him, focusing on the curve of his buttocks in his jeans. The T-shirt was a little too small, riding up on his back so I could see the dimples in his lower back just above the swell of his ass. He was a little more slender than I liked, but it didn't matter since I wasn't going to fuck him. I was just going to pierce his neck for a moment and drink from his veins until the desire faded and I returned to my normal state.

*You haven't been normal in over two years*, a voice whispered inside my head.

I ignored it as always.

He crossed St. Ann Street and continued on his way up Chartres, still talking on the phone, completely oblivious to everything and everyone around him. There weren't many people about on Chartres Street as darkness continued to fall on the Quarter. I felt power surging through my body with each step I took. The darkness is the vampire's friend, making us even more powerful, stronger. My eyes adjusted to the darkness. At first the clarity of my night vision always caught me off guard, but now I was used to it. I started walking faster, figuring I could catch up to him and pull him into one of the many shadowed doorways. Anyone passing by would assume we were simply enjoying a public display of affection—and the groans of pleasure he would emit as I drained off some of his blood would give further proof to the lie.

The blood scent was so strong I could almost taste it, the need rising in me, and I knew I had to catch him soon—

"Cord?"

I froze, stopped walking.

"My God, it *is* you." A hand grabbed my arm from behind and spun me around. "I—I thought you were *dead*, man."

"Let me go." I growled, the need beginning to push everything else out of my mind, and I was dangerously close to losing control.

"No way, man!" My old roommate from Beta Kappa, Jared Holcomb, was smiling at me. His entire face lit up with the smile the way it always had. His thick blond hair was longer than I remembered it being, and his muscles were thicker, stronger. He was wearing a tight pair of low-rise jeans and a tight blue shirt that hugged his torso. "Where have you been? My God…I'm so glad to see you!"

*Always feed before the desire becomes need, my maker, Jean-Paul, had lectured me, over and over again. When it becomes need, you cannot control yourself and you will take risks you usually don't, you put yourself at risk.*

It was too late.

I grabbed Jared with both hands and pulled him into an unlit doorway, wrapping my arms around him and pressing my body up against his. He made a shocked noise, squirming a bit before I sank my teeth into his neck and drank.

I could feel my cock hardening. I could feel his hardening against mine as he began to moan as the delicious warm blood filled my mouth from the little wounds I'd made, as his precious life force entered my body.

I pulled my head back, wiping at my mouth, gasping.

Jared remained leaning against the door, his breath coming in shallow gulps. His eyes were half-closed, and blood was dribbling down his neck from the holes I'd left in his throat. I took a few steps back and checked the street. There was no one nearby, no one closer than Jackson Square a half block away.

"Fuck," I muttered under my breath. I'd gotten lucky. I shook my head, furious at myself. What if he hadn't been alone? What if someone had come walking along at just the right moment, or a police car had come around the corner at St. Ann just as I grabbed him?

*When desire becomes need, a vampire forgets everything but the blood. He makes mistakes, takes risks he shouldn't—and frequently gets caught. It must never become need, else you risk everything. Most vampires are caught—and killed—*

*when they've gone too long without feeding. Don't let that happen to you.*

I must have been crazy to let it go so long—especially when there were always people about in the Quarter to feed on. What had I been thinking?

*You weren't thinking, that's the problem*, I scolded myself. *Seeing how long you could go? That's madness, and a one-way ticket to death.*

I shook my head again, then pricked my right index finger with one of my teeth and rubbed my blood over the two little holes the way Jean-Paul had shown me.

The holes didn't close the way they usually did.

I stared at the wounds. It couldn't be. They *always* healed.

I could feel the panic rising in me as I rubbed more of my blood over the punctures. I heard myself muttering "come on, come on, come on" over and over again, but the wounds weren't healing the way they were supposed to. Instead, Jared's blood continued to seep slowly out through them, dribbling down his neck and staining his shirt. The pale blue was turning dark just below the collar, where the running blood came into contact with the tightly fitting cotton. His nipples were erect, and all of his weight was leaning back against the wall. His eyes opened a little wider yet were still half-closed. Other than the bleeding neck, his eyes looked like so many others who drank more than they should in the Quarter. They weren't focused and looked a little cloudy to me. "What"—he swallowed, his throat working, the Adam's apple bobbing up and down—"wha—happen? Cord? I feel—I feel funny."

I couldn't just leave him there, with his neck bleeding and his shirt getting darker with wetness every passing second. Something was wrong, something was seriously wrong, and I had to get away as quickly as I could, but I couldn't just leave him there.

Modern society might not believe in vampires, but when the police found him—and he would certainly wind up in the hands of the police—they might not go for the notion of a vampire attack, but I couldn't take the risk he would remember seeing me and mention me to the cops.

And since Cord Logan had died in a fire two years earlier on Lundi Gras, that was a can of worms best left unopened.

I put his left arm around my shoulders and placed his head down on my neck. At least the wounds were hidden that way, and in the growing darkness maybe no one would notice the bloody shirt. "Come on, buddy, you need to walk with me," I whispered to him.

His head tilted back for a moment and his face lit up with a crazy grin. "Cord, buddy. I knew you weren't dead. I tole them all you weren't dead."

"Come on, it's just a couple of blocks." I smiled into his eyes, willing him to start walking. "Use me for support if you can't stand up."

"Okay, buddy," he replied, and started walking. Most of his weight was on me, and had I been a mortal, we probably would have both fallen to the ground. But I was no longer mortal, and while I had not matured into my full strength as a vampire—Jean-Paul said it would take another fifty or so mortal years for that to happen—I was still stronger than I'd been when I was a twenty-year-old college student. We shuffled our way past the Presbytere, no one really paying any attention to us. It was a common sight in the Quarter—Jared looked like another young man who'd had too much to drink and needed to be helped back to his hotel. We turned and headed down the alley between the Presbytere and the Cathedral. The alley was empty and silent other than our footsteps against the stone. Even though I was stronger, I was still having trouble drawing breath by the time we reached Royal Street. We headed up Orleans, past the crowds on Bourbon and the dancing hand grenade in front of Tropical Isle, and before I knew it we were climbing the steps of Jean-Paul's house. I put the key in the lock and helped him inside, setting him down on the couch.

As I turned to shut and lock the front door I stared at the little cottage across the street. It was still in the process of being rebuilt after the fire. It was there that Jean-Paul had rescued me from the witch Sebastian, and brought my dying body back across the street to his house. It was on that very couch where Jared now lay that Jean-Paul had opened the vein in his arm and had me drink his blood, the blood that transformed me into what I am now, no longer human. I shut the door and drew the curtains shut, flipping the light switch. The overhead chandelier came to life, casting strange shadows into every corner.

I knelt down beside Jared. His eyes were now fully closed and his breathing was shallow. His skin felt cold, and I pressed my fingers against his wrist. His heart was beating, but not strongly. The wounds on his neck had stopped bleeding but still were open and angry. I put my hand up to my mouth in order to open another wound in a finger but stopped.

*Think about it, Cord, you must be doing something wrong. You've done this before a thousand times and it always, always works.*

But as much as I thought about it, hard as I tried to remember, there was nothing else I could remember doing differently I wasn't doing now. It was very simple—you merely opened a wound and rubbed some of your own blood over the mortal's wounds. Within seconds, those wounds would close just as your own would. I shook my head and punctured my thumb.

I pressed my thumb over his wounds, rubbed gently, and pulled my thumb away. Even as the wound in my own thumb closed, the wounds in Jared's neck remained clearly visible.

I took a deep breath and tried not to panic.

Jared opened his eyes again and smiled weakly. "Cord, buddy. I knew you weren't dead." He reached up with a cool hand and touched the side of my face. "I just knew. Everyone said you were dead, they had a funeral and everything, but I knew." His face clouded with confusion. "But how…I don't understand…"

"Shh," I whispered, my mind racing as I tried to figure out what to do.

This was precisely why Jean-Paul had forbidden me to return to New Orleans. He was right again, as usual. *Yes, I know you're not from there, but you do know people who are, and they all think you're dead. You cannot risk going back there. What are you going to do if one of them sees you? How are you going to explain being alive? There is no explanation, Cord, and you will have to kill them.*

And even though Jared had been one of my best friends, one of my fraternity brothers, I knew if Jean-Paul knew what was happening, he would order me to kill Jared. Kill him and make sure the body was never found.

*If you don't kill him, you risk exposing yourself. And everyone else in the vampire world—is that what you want, Cord? To prove to them vampires DO exist? They would hunt us all down and kill us. It's either him or us, Cord. You know what you have to do.*

"I feel funny," Jared said, shifting around on the couch, and his eyes opened even further. They weren't as glassy and unfocused as they had been earlier; that was a step in the right direction.

Maybe he would recover normally.

I placed my fingers back on his wrist. His pulse felt stronger.

The wounds on his neck were scabbing over.

*That's a step in the right direction, but it's still not normal. My blood should have healed the damned things! What's wrong? Maybe Jared is somehow different than other humans?*

*But that doesn't make any sense.*

"Kiss me," Jared whispered, smiling at me.

"What?" I stared at him. "You can't be serious."

"I want you," he whispered. His lips spread in a smile. "I've always wanted you, Cord. Always."

I gulped. In the three years at Ole Miss I'd known Jared, I'd never once gotten the slightest inkling he was gay, or even the least bit curious. We'd pledged together, shared a room at the house, and been as close as brothers. Jared was the only person in the house I'd come out to—and he'd been supportive, even going with me to Memphis to a gay bar. It had been Jared's idea to come stay with his parents for Mardi Gras, and he'd helped me break away from the other fraternity brothers who'd also come down so I could go to the gay bars. Neither of us had any way of knowing the trip would result in my becoming a vampire—well, Jared just thought I'd been killed, burned to death in the fire. I'd always been attracted to Jared, but never considered acting on it—no matter how drunk or high either one of us might have been.

And it was very tempting.

"Jared—"

"I mean it." He licked his lips. "I was too much of a coward to ever do anything. That time we went to the bar in

Memphis…I wanted to kiss you that night. It broke my heart when you died, Cord. And now you're alive. I'm not going to miss this chance. I've been sorry ever since you died I never had the courage to do anything with you." He smiled again. "But now you aren't dead." He reached out and touched my hair. "Somehow, I knew you weren't. I knew that wasn't you in that house."

Tears filled my eyes. Oh, how I'd longed to hear those words from him! How I'd longed to kiss him, to put my arms around him, to put my mouth on his cock, to let him fill me up with his. But this didn't feel right somehow, it was wrong, like somehow my biting him and sucking his blood had done this to him—was making him think and react in a way that wasn't natural to him.

But his wounds hadn't healed. That wasn't natural, either.

He leaned up and kissed me.

It felt like an electrical current ran through my body.

Not even kissing Jean-Paul had felt like this.

I felt my cock growing hard inside my jeans, and as Jared's tongue slipped between my lips and inside my mouth, I could see in my head that he was getting hard too. I reached down and caressed the thick hardness beneath the denim, and he moaned, never removing his tongue from inside my mouth. He stroked my chest, pulling and tweaking at my erect and sensitive nipples, and I pushed him back down on the couch, climbing on top of him, our hips beginning to move back and forth as we ground our crotches into each other.

I pulled my mouth away from his lips. He smiled up at me. "I love you, Cord," he breathed, "I always have."

*Jean-Paul never said that to me.*

I wanted to believe him.

But still, in spite of how badly I wanted him, the animalistic need driving me, I couldn't shake the sense that something, somehow, was not right about this.

His hands came up, caressing my hardness through my pants, and my desire pushed all other thoughts out of my mind.

I reached down and undid my pants, freeing my cock. He smiled up at me and licked his thumb. He started running it over the head of my cock.

"Ooooooh," I moaned.

I pushed my pants down as he kept rubbing away. Unable to stand it anymore, I grabbed the front of his pants and pulled, the riveted buttons holding his fly closed popping and flying away. I got to my knees and yanked his pants down, freeing his long, beautiful cock. As I yanked I heard the denim tearing and once the pants were free I tossed them aside like torn rags. I reached for the bottle of lube and squirted it onto his erection.

"I want to be inside you," he breathed as I mounted him, spreading my butt cheeks and lowering myself on top of his cock.

The pressure against my anus was sharp and painful, then my muscles relaxed and I slid down, feeling his urgency filling me. I gasped and moaned as I continued to slide, settling down onto him when I felt his thick balls pressing against my cheeks.

His entire body began to tremble, his eyes closing partway as I started moving up and down. He tried to push up into me as I went upward, but I held his hips down with my hands. He struggled against my strength at first, to no avail. I was much stronger than he—he had no idea how strong, nor did I want him to find out. I was still not completely used to how much power my muscles now contained, and I was afraid if we started struggling I might accidentally hurt him.

"Your ass is amazing," he whispered, tugging on my nipples and sending electricity through my body. "It feels so good, please don't stop."

I smiled. The pleasure was so intense I couldn't stop had I wanted to. I reached down and stroked his chest, and his entire body convulsed, bucking upward. The thrusts were strong, intense, and it felt as though I was being split in two.

I cried out, my head going back as he continued driving up into me. My entire mind was consumed with the pleasure from his cock, which felt as though it were burning inside me. No one had ever fucked me this way, not Jean-Paul, not any of the others in our little fraternity of vampires. The passion, the power—my eyes began to lose focus, and everything in front of me seemed to be seared with white, and I was vaguely aware that he was forcing me backward, never stopping with the thrusting, not once relenting, and the pleasure, my God, the pleasure, and I was on my back and he was on top of me, and in the mirror behind him I could see his powerful back, the fleur-de-lis tattoo on his right shoulder blade, his beautiful round white ass clenching and unclenching as he drove into me, as though he were trying to get his cock so deep inside me it might never come out, and I wanted him inside me, I wanted to feel his entire body consumed inside mine, and the thrusting and driving to never stop...

And his lips were at my throat, moving from the base of my chin to the hollow where my neck met my chest, his tongue darting out and dancing against my skin.

And it went on, the pleasure building inside me until I could barely stand it any longer—

And his head went back and he screamed as his body

went rigid, and I could feel him squirting inside me, his body convulsing and racking with the pleasure with each spurt—

And my own splashed out of me, raining onto my chest and my face and into my hair.

He convulsed a few more times, then collapsed on top of me, his energy spent.

I lay there panting for a moment or two, enjoying his weight and warmth on top of me.

His breathing shallowed and became even, and I gently pushed him aside, feeling his softening penis slide out of me. I slid out and gently rolled him over onto his back, staring at his beauty as he lay there in the soft glow of moonlight coming through the stained glass just above the front door of the house.

Blood still oozed from the wounds on his neck.

I grabbed a towel and wiped myself off, then spat onto my fingers. I rubbed them over the wounds, but again, the wounds did not close.

*I don't understand, it has always worked, what is wrong, what is so different about this time that the wounds will not close?*

He started murmuring in his sleep, tossing a bit on the couch.

I walked over to the front windows and opened the red velvet curtains a bit, looking at the house across the street—the house where I'd almost died, a victim of the desires of the mixed-race witch, Sebastian, and his thirst to combine the power of the vampire with his own witchcraft. I closed my eyes and remembered being tied to the bed while Sebastian violated my body and went through the mysterious ritual I had not understood until Jean-Paul and the others had come to my rescue. I remembered the feeling of dying, of my body going cold as Jean-Paul wrapped me in a blanket and carried me out of the house and back across the street, and the metallic taste of his blood as he fed me in order to save me.

I tried to remember if my own initial wounds from him had closed that first night he had fed from me, that night when I'd run into him and his friends at Oz while the madness of Carnival raged in the streets of the French Quarter.

*Perhaps I took too much from him. Maybe that's why the wounds wouldn't heal. Jean-Paul and the others always warned me about taking too much—but they never said why.*

I started to turn away from the window when something flickered in one of the windows across the street. I spun my head back, but whatever it was, was no longer there.

*Now you're imagining things. There's no one there, the house isn't habitable yet.*

Jared moaned in his sleep, and I walked back over to the couch. I knelt down beside him and marveled again at just how beautiful he was.

I'd always had a bit of a crush on him back at the fraternity house, but he was straight—he'd made that very clear to me.

*Then why did he—it doesn't make any sense. Was it the connection forged when I took his blood? His life force? There's so much you still don't know about all of this, Jean-Paul was right, you should have stayed in Palm Springs with him and the others.*

I reached over and stroked his brow. He shifted again, and his eyes opened. I recoiled—they were no longer blue, but rather brown.

He smiled at me. "Sebastian does not rest, Cord."

My hand froze on his forehead. "You don't know that, Jared, you couldn't possibly know that." *How does he even know about Sebastian in the first place? And what is wrong with his eyes?*

His eyes closed and he moaned. When they reopened, they were clearly blue. I must have imagined what I'd seen. Besides, it didn't make any sense. Eyes couldn't change color like that, could they?

"I don't feel so good," he barely whispered as I started stroking his forehead again. "What—what have you done to me, Cord?" He shifted again on the couch. "So cold, so very very cold."

I allowed my other hand to come up and press on the jugular vein in his throat. The heartbeat was weak and faint.

*I've killed him.*

I felt tears rising in my eyes.

I raised my wrist to my mouth and bit into the artery there. As my own blood began to flow over my skin, I lowered my wrist to his mouth.

I heard Jean-Paul's voice in my head. *You are too young to this life to create another such as ourselves. Your heart isn't strong enough yet, so you must never ever try to turn a human until such time as I tell you that you can.*

But he would die unless…

"Drink," I whispered, parting his lips and allowing my blood to run onto his tongue.

Jared's eyes opened at the first taste of my blood, and color began to return to his cheeks. He closed his mouth around the holes in my wrist and began to suckle.

I closed my eyes and allowed my head to fall backward.

Whatever the risks, I had to take them.

## SOMEONE TO LAY DOWN BESIDE ME

Y ou *really* see some tragic drag in this place at four in the morning," Dennis said, shaking his head. He said it a little too loudly, and I glanced over at the counter nervously. He rolled his eyes and smiled at me. "Don't look so worried. She didn't hear me." He looked over at her with disgust on his face. "Besides, she's so fucking wasted she doesn't know what day it is."

He plucked a packet of Sweet'n Low out of the little caddy next to the ketchup and mustard bottles and shook it a few times before dumping it into his red plastic cup of iced tea. He took a big swig before using a paper napkin to wipe beads of sweat off his forehead.

It wasn't quite four in the morning, but I wasn't going to be sleeping anytime soon. The digital jukebox was blasting a remix of Rihanna—"Only Girl in the World," which weirdly enough seemed like the appropriate soundtrack for the episode of *The Real Housewives from Hell* playing on the flat-screen television mounted on the wall I was facing.

I wiped my own forehead with a napkin. It was hot in the Clover Grill and the air seemed thick and heavy with grease. Burgers were frying on the grill, and French fries were sizzling in the deep fryer. The smell was making me more than a little nauseous. I didn't know how Dennis could possibly eat anything. I felt a wave of nausea coming on, so I closed my eyes and took some deep breaths till it passed. My lower back was aching, so I turned in my chair and put my back up against the wall. We were sitting at the table in the absolute back, and Dennis had his back to the front door. I put my feet up on the extra chair at our table and leaned forward a bit, trying to stretch the ache out of my back.

I took another big drink out of my red plastic cup of water and couldn't help smiling to myself. I recognized the tragic-looking drag queen sitting at the counter. I'd seen Floretta Flynn perform any number of times at various clubs in the Quarter. She was one of the better drag performers in the city and was actually quite funny. She'd been hostess of the show we'd caught earlier in the evening at the Parade while we were waiting for our dealer to show up. She'd clearly had too much to drink since then—Dennis swore drag queens were always smashed when they went onstage, but I couldn't tell. It was obvious now, though. She was seated at the counter on one of the revolving stools, leaning against a hot muscle boy who didn't seem quite as wasted as she was. Her massive 1970s country-singer wig was askew and her lipstick was smeared around her mouth. Her mascara was also smudged around her eyes, and it looked like she might have tried to wipe off some of the foundation and rouge on her cheeks. Her bright red sequined dress looked dirty, and she'd spilled something down the front of it.

"The wreck of the *Hesperides*," I replied in a much lower voice, just in case she had some kind of bat-like hearing.

"Drag queens also should always avoid direct overhead lighting." Dennis shrugged. "Even when their makeup is fresh it isn't pretty. Don't they teach that in drag school?" He rolled his eyes and took another swig of his tea. "I'd think that would be Drag 101."

I gulped out of my water glass. My buzz was already wearing off. I hadn't drunk much—a couple of mixed drinks, a bottle of Bud Light, at most—and we'd smoked a joint on the balcony, but it had been enough to alter my mood. But the energy in the club had been off—it seemed like there had been far too many drunken straight girls at Oz, the ones who come to gay bars to show how cool they are and make complete fools out of themselves in the process. One had sloshed some of her drink on me on the dance floor, and if I'd had a dime for every time one of them almost burned me with the lit cigarette she carelessly waved around like it was an accessory, I'd never have to worry about where my next meal was coming from ever again. So when Dennis finally said "the hell with this" and suggested getting something to eat at the Clover, I was more than happy to put my shirt back on and follow him out the front door of Oz.

*If I'd only known those stupid drunk bitches were going to be there*, I thought as I looked around, *I wouldn't have wasted my time or my money there.*

The problem was I was still horny—and the likelihood of getting laid was getting smaller by the minute.

The Clover Grill was pretty empty. Floretta and her muscle boy were the only people at the counter. Besides a group of large and extremely hairy bears at the front table, we were the only people in the whole place.

I adjusted my shorts again and wondered if Dennis would be up for some meaningless sex. I narrowed my eyes and watched him worrying his straw. He was looking out the picture window across the street at Lafitte's, which was also pretty deserted. A drop of sweat had pooled in the hollow at the base of his throat.

He was so fucking hot. He was wearing a Saints baseball cap backward—he always claimed it wasn't to hide his receding hairline, but methinks he doth protest too much—and his features were strong enough to pull the look off. He had enormous, expressive brown eyes, a square jaw, and thick, eminently kissable lips. His years teaching aerobics and working as a personal trainer had given him a thickly muscled yet defined body. His tight white tank top showed off his dark tan. His arms were crisscrossed with bulging veins. He turned his head back toward me and smiled. He was one of the few people I'd ever known who smiled with his entire face.

My balls ached.

I opened my mouth to ask, but before I could form the words he yawned and said, "All I want to do is eat and go home and take a Xanax and sleep till Monday." He took the ball cap off and ran his hand through his sweaty hair, smiling at me again as he put the cap back on. "Probably just as well the night was so off," he went on, "who knows what trouble we might have gotten into?" He winked at me.

This was the kind of mixed signal he'd always given me, the kind that had always made me think there was a chance of something more between us than just being friends. I closed my eyes and decided to not bring it up. Even though I knew it wouldn't mean a damned thing other than two friends scratching an itch, I couldn't forget the one time it had happened.

Dennis would think I was still hung up on him if I suggested it, had backslid, or worse, had never ever gotten over him in the first place.

And to be honest, as hot as Dennis was, the sex wouldn't be worth dealing with all of that shit the next morning.

*Fuck it, after I eat my fries I'll head down to the bathhouse and fuck someone there*, I decided. Dennis didn't approve of anonymous sex in bathhouses, so I'd have to walk him back to his place and pretend like I was going home. I glanced at my watch. A little before four—I could be there by five, and hopefully pounding someone's ass by five fifteen. By then all the guys coming down from their drugs but not ready to go home yet would be there—and wanting it bad.

"Are you still high?" Dennis shrugged his shoulders. "Mine wore off a while ago." He made a face. "What a shitty night—we should have just stayed home and watched movies or something." He frowned as a couple of guys walked past the big window in the direction of Esplanade Avenue. They looked slightly familiar—but I didn't get a good look. The scowl on Dennis's face, though, let me know he knew and didn't like one or both of them. "Last weekend sucked too," he went on as our waiter put a plate of French fries in front of me and a grilled chicken sandwich down in front of him. "And tonight was a total waste of money."

"No shit," I replied. "It's not like I've got a lot of extra cash to throw away." I closed my eyes and tilted my head back against the tiled wall. I didn't get paid again until Wednesday—and I thought I had exactly forty bucks in the bank and no food in my apartment. *Should've just stayed home tonight, found someone online*, I lectured myself. *Ah, well, I still have credit on my card—I can use that for the bathhouse and some groceries. Yeah, should've stayed home and found a trick online...stupid stupid stupid.*

I opened my mouth to say something else when I realized the guy with Floretta was looking at me. Our eyes met, and he smiled at me.

I was dazzled as he stood up and stretched.

He was a blond, with his hair cut close to the scalp in a military style that emphasized his square jaw, strong nose, and wide mouth. He had blue eyes and was wearing a pair of khaki shorts that reached his knees. His red T-shirt had the sleeves cut off deeply, so that his entire side was exposed. He grinned at me with dimples cutting deep into his tanned cheeks. His arms were huge, as were his shoulder muscles. Veins stood out on his arms, and his waist was narrow—he was widely built from the front, but from the side his waist looked tiny. His pecs were big, and his shirt clung to his big, hard nipples. He walked along the counter toward our table. He kept smiling at me as he walked. I knew Dennis was still talking between bites of his sandwich, but all I heard was mumbling. The loud music from the jukebox was nothing more than white noise in the background as he walked slowly toward where I was sitting, that big smile still on his face.

God, my cock ached.

He walked past us, and I turned to watch him go out the door to the courtyard, where the bathrooms were. His back was broad, and the muscles twitched beneath the tanned skin pulled tightly across them. His ass was round and full—not as big as maybe I would prefer, but it would definitely do. For a brief second I pictured him underneath me, smiling that big grin up at me while I slid my dick into his ass—

"Earth to Gary? Are you there, Gary?" Dennis waved his hand in front of my face and, to add insult to injury, snapped his fingers.

Irritated, I pushed his hand away from my face. "Don't do that," I said. "You know I hate it when you do that."

He smirked at me. "That's pretty, all right. Why don't you go say hello? Introduce yourself?" There was a taunting tone to his voice that made me want to smack him.

I started to snap back at him, but stopped myself. Instead, I smiled at him and said, "You know, I think I will." I got out of my chair and walked out the side door and through the courtyard to the bathroom. Once in the courtyard, I leaned against the side of the building and closed my eyes. *Idiot, idiot, idiot*, I moaned. I never had the nerve to actually approach anyone—especially not someone as hot as this guy. But my dick was still semi-hard, and my balls were still aching. I was about to turn and walk back inside the diner when I heard the bathroom door's bolt being slid back, and it opened.

I opened my eyes as he walked out of the bathroom.

Our eyes met, and he smiled. "Hey."

"Hey," I replied, stepping out of his way.

But instead of going back inside, he just stood there smiling at me. It seemed like we stood there in the moonlight staring at each for an eternity before he finally said, "My name's Trey." He stuck out his hand, which I stared at stupidly for a moment before taking.

His hand was warm, enormous and strong. "Gary," I said, feeling like a complete idiot.

"Nice to meet you." He didn't let go of my hand. "Don't you have to go to the bathroom?"

"Actually, no." I heard the words coming out before I could stop them. "I followed you out here." I was mortified—I certainly didn't want him to think I cruised bathrooms in public places.

Before I knew what was happening, he pulled me in closer and kissed me briefly on the mouth. His big thick arms went around me, and his hands cupped my ass.

Our crotches brushed against each other, and I could feel his hardness.

I pulled my head back and whispered, "Um, you want to come back to my place?"

He nuzzled my neck. "How far is it?"

"Not far. Just about a block."

He licked his lips. "Works for me—if you want to."

I let my hand brush against his crotch. "I don't want to make out here in the Clover Grill's courtyard," I replied, although I'd done much worse in more public places before. "Come on."

I took him by the hand and led him back into the grill, pausing at the table long enough to give Dennis a five for my fries. I didn't wait for him to say anything—but he had that judgmental look on his face that always pissed me off. Trey kissed Floretta on her makeup-smudged cheek, and she gave me a crooked, approving grin. Trey took my hand again and led me outside. Once outside on Dumaine Street, he walked alongside me as we headed up to Dauphine. "Your friend didn't look too happy," Trey said over the music blaring out of Lafitte's as we walked past.

"Dennis—Dennis thinks I'm a slut," I replied.

Trey laughed. "And he's not?"

I stopped walking. "You haven't slept with him, have you?"

He laughed again and shook his head. "No—would it matter if I had?" He pushed me up against the side of a house and kissed me long and hard again. When he pulled back, I gasped out, "No."

When we reached the side gate at my place, he kissed the back of my neck as I fit my key into the lock and turned it.

I barely had time to flip the light switch just inside my front door when he pushed me against the wall and hungrily kissed me, his tongue probing inside my mouth. I sucked his tongue, refusing to let it go and making him keep kissing me as I fumbled with the button of his jeans, finally getting them open. I pushed his jeans down while we still kissed, and grabbed hold of his bare ass with both hands as he put his hands into my armpits and lifted me easily. I let his tongue go and gasped while he kept me up in the air. I wrapped my legs around his waist, and he held me there as he pulled his jeans up so he could walk—and headed over to the couch, where he gently lowered me down onto my back. He pulled his T-shirt up over his head and I couldn't help but stare at his smooth torso, the big heavy pecs, the huge round erect nipples, the ripples in his flat stomach as he kicked his shoes off and slid the pants down and off, standing there over me, his long hard cock standing out away from the golden pubic hair. He straddled me, a knee on either side of my rib cage, and I leaned up and licked the end of his cock.

He moaned as I started sucking—no, worshiping—his cock. It was magnificent, the skin soft and smooth and hot, tasting of salty sweat and smelling of musky manhood as my mouth moved slowly up and down its shaft, my free hand cupping and gently squeezing his thick, heavy, shaved balls as I slurped away at this amazing rod. I ran my other hand up his torso, tweaking a nipple before sliding down the ridges of his abs, and I opened my eyes, looking straight up at him. His head was tilted back, so I could just see the straight line of his throat, and still I worked on his cock, teasing the slit with my tongue while he emitted guttural groans of delight from deep inside his diaphragm.

He pushed my head away, and I looked at him, puzzled.

He simply smiled and got off the couch.

He grabbed my shirt with both hands and yanked hard, lifting me up off the cushions. I heard the fabric tear as he kept pulling, and then the fabric gave way completely and tore free. He tossed my shredded shirt aside like it was nothing and undid my jeans, sliding them down and off me, tossing them over his shoulder. He tore my underwear off me.

The sound of it ripping in his hands and the feel of my hard cock springing free was so hot, so arousing, I would have let him fuck me right then and there.

Instead, he got down on all fours on the couch, facing away from me, and backed up until his balls and cock were in my face. He leaned down and took mine in his mouth, and I reached up and started licking the underside of his balls before moving on to his cock.

The feel of his tongue, of his warm wet mouth, on me was so intense I thought I might come—which I certainly didn't want. I didn't want this to ever stop. It was incredible.

I started trembling and let his cock slip away from my mouth as I took some deep breaths to keep the wave of pleasure from overwhelming me.

But *he* was still working away on my dick, and oh my God it felt—

Amazing.

So good I didn't know if I could handle it.

Like the top of my head was going to blow right off.

I turned my head to one side and bit my lip as tears filled my eyes, as joy swept through my body, and I tentatively stuck my tongue out and let the tip touch his thigh.

His skin tasted salty, and I licked his thigh again, tracing little circles while waves of pleasure crashed over me.

I was barely aware as he stopped what he was doing, but I noticed when he moved out of range of my tongue.

I opened my eyes and looked up into his eyes. He smiled at me, and I fell into the deep blue of his eyes, and it was like we were merging into one person as his lips touched my throat, his hands pinching my nipples, and it was so incredibly arousing, it felt so fucking good, no one had ever driven me so wild with desire before, and I wanted him, I wanted to be part of him, I wanted our skin to meld together so we would be one creature, one combined, and I felt the head of his cock teasing my asshole and I was so deep in his eyes I couldn't resist him, and he started to slide inside me and I couldn't draw breath, I couldn't breathe, all I could do was gasp as his tongue traced along my throat up to my earlobe and then the lobe was between his teeth and he was nibbling taking little bites all the while his fingers were pinching and tweaking and pulling my nipples and I wanted to scream it felt so good but I was so deep inside his eyes I was afraid if I made any sound, any sound at all it might deafen him cause him to pull back cause him to withdraw from me and we would separate and I didn't want that I didn't want that at all I wanted him to be a part of me I wanted to be a part of him and I could feel some pressure inside me as he pushed against me yet his tongue and lips never stopped moving and my nipples my god my nipples he was pulling and twisting and working them no one had ever worked them quite that way before oh my god what was he doing to me I never wanted him to stop—

"You're high, aren't you?" he whispered in my ear, and his breath tickled my skin, sending a tingle through my body that didn't stop until it reached my toes and went out into the universe from there, and his voice echoed inside my head.

"A little bit," I answered, and I looked into his blue eyes and was lost in them, into the beautiful deep azure, and then his lips were on my throat again, his teeth taking little bites out of my skin. As another wave of pleasure washed over my body I wanted him to take me into his mouth. I wanted him in my mouth again, and I reached down and wrapped my hand around his thick cock. "Fuck me, please," I heard myself saying, "I want you inside me," and before I knew what was happening he had pushed me down and was between my legs, pushing them up, and the head of his cock was pushing inside me.

It felt like I was being torn in half but it was good, it felt right, like it was how I was meant to be, like I'd been born for this one moment, and I closed my eyes, tilted my head back, and gave myself over to the pleasure.

Wave after wave coursed through my body as he slowly

fucked me, sliding his dick in and out of me in a rhythm intended to push me to my limits. My body was trembling uncontrollably as he worked my ass, his big hands tweaking my nipples, and I could feel drops of precome working their way up my own cock, dripping out of the slit onto my abs as he kept pushing and pulling inside me, occasionally stopping to let me experience the feeling of being completely filled by him.

I tried to breathe but I was gasping as my body shook, yet he still didn't move. I looked up at him and he was smiling at me. I watched a drop of sweat run down from his forehead down his nose. It hung there for just a moment on the tip before dropping onto me. I felt it splash on my chest, and I reached up with both hands to grab his thick pecs. His smile didn't waver, he didn't move, he was still shoved all the way inside me as he raised both of his arms and flexed his biceps muscles, veins thickening over them and in his forearms, his chest hardening under my hands as I kept squeezing them, and I wanted him to start fucking me again, harder and nastier, I wanted him to shove inside me so hard I'd move, so I start twisting under him as another drop of sweat flowed down his nose, beads of water forming in the deep canyon between his chest muscles, his tanned skin glistening in the light.

"Oh, you want me to fuck you some more?" he asked, his low, deep voice getting under my skin, the words echoing inside my head.

"Fuck me," I hissed, my eyes narrowing as I tried to move. "Pound me, make me your little slut pig bitch, come on, stud, give it to me!"

His smile faded, and his lips curled into a sneer as he slid slowly out of me.

I gasped.

When all that was left inside me was the head, he snarled, "Beg for it."

My body was trembling with need and desire.

He twisted both of my nipples. "Beg, you fucking bitch."

He kept twisting as I gasped, and the shock of the pain turned to pleasure.

It was like my nipples were wired directly to my balls.

He slammed all the way into me before I could say a word, before I could react to anything.

The intensity of the pleasure overwhelmed me and I screamed.

I bucked upward, my upper body rising, but he roughly planted his hands on my chest and slammed me back down on my back.

Now he was pounding, slamming into me so fast that I couldn't even gasp. It felt so good, but his thrusts were coming so quickly I didn't have time to moan or groan or make any noise other than the gasps as I tried to suck in air before he slammed into me again and drove it all back out of me.

Come shot out of my cock, splashing on my chest, my stomach, hitting me in the face.

And still, he kept pounding on me.

Sweat rolled down his face, his chest glistened wetly as he grunted from the exertion.

I grabbed his nipples and pulled.

His head went back and he screamed.

I could feel his cock jerking with each spurt inside me.

With each jerk of his cock he howled again, his body shaking.

His eyes were still closed.

Finally, he stopped.

He slowly slid out of me and smiled down at me.

He bent over me and licked my come off me.

"You have an awesome ass, man," he said, running his hand through his wet hair.

I made room for him beside me on the couch, and he dropped down, sliding an arm under my head. He was on his side, and I slid over until our wet skin was touching.

"I don't usually—I don't usually get fucked," I replied, resting my head against his chest and listening to his heartbeat.

"It felt so good I didn't want to come," he said. He pressed his lips against my forehead. "Sorry if I was rough."

"I liked it," I replied, a knowing smile coming onto my face. I turned and faced him. "You could have gotten rougher."

"Let me rest for a bit, and then I'll show you rough."

I reached down and grabbed his dick. "Let's go into the bedroom."

I got up off the couch and led him back to my bed. As he lay down on the bed I glanced out the window.

Dennis was sitting on a chair outside his apartment door, and I wondered if he'd heard us.

A smile crossed my face. I didn't care if he did, and why should I? He'd made it clear more than once that I wasn't his boyfriend, would never be. What right did he have to judge me?

I nestled inside Trey's big arm and rested my head on his sweaty chest. It felt good.

It felt right.

"Whenever you're ready," I whispered as I lay down next to him. "Sir."

# About the Author

Todd Gregory is a New Orleans–based writer who survived Hurricane Katrina and its aftermath with the help of prescription medication. He has edited the anthologies *Rough Trade*, *Wings*, *Sweat*, and *Blood Sacraments*. Todd has published short stories in numerous anthologies, and his works have been translated into German and Spanish. He has also published three novels (*Every Frat Boy Wants It*, *Games Frat Boys Play*, *Need*) and is currently at work on his fourth.

# Books Available From Bold Strokes Books

**Straight Boy Roommate** by Kevin Troughton. Tom isn't expecting much from his first term at University, but a chance encounter with straight boy Dan catapults him into an extraordinary, wild weekend of sex and self-discovery, which turns his life upside down, and leads him into his first love affair. (978-1-60282-782-0)

**Raising Hell: Demonic Gay Erotica**, edited by Todd Gregory. Hot stories of gay erotica featuring demons. (978-1-60282-768-4)

**Pursued** by Joel Gomez-Dossi. Openly gay college student Jamie Bradford becomes romantically involved with two men at the same time, and his hell begins when one of his boyfriends becomes intent on killing him. (978-1-60282-769-1)

**Timothy** by Greg Herren. Timothy is a romantic suspense thriller from award-winning mystery writer Greg Herren set in the fabulous Hamptons. (978-1-60282-760-8)

**In Stone** by Jeremy Jordan King. A young New Yorker is rescued from a hate crime by a mysterious someone who turns out to be more of a something. (978-1-60282-761-5)

**The Jesus Injection** by Eric Andrews-Katz. Murderous statues, demented drag queens, political bombings, ex-gay ministries, espionage, and romance are all in a day's work for a top secret agent. But the gloves are off when Agent Buck 98 comes up against the Jesus Injection. (978-1-60282-762-2)

**Combustion** by Daniel W. Kelly. Bearish detective Deck Waxer comes to the city of Kremfort Cove to investigate why the hottest men in town are bursting into flames in broad daylight. (978-1-60282-763-9)

**Night Shadows: Queer Horror** edited by Greg Herren and J.M. Redmann. *Night Shadows* features delightfully wicked stories by some of the biggest names in queer publishing. (978-1-60282-751-6)

**Wyatt: Doc Holliday's Account of an Intimate Friendship** by Dale Chase. Erotica writer Dale Chase takes the remarkable friendship between Wyatt Earp, upright lawman, and Doc Holliday, Southern gentlemen turned gambler and killer, to an entirely new level: hot! (978-1-60282-755-4)

**Secret Societies** by William Holden. An outcast hustler, his unlikely "mother," his faithless lovers, and his religious persecutors—all in 1726. (978-1-60282-752-3)

**The Jetsetters** by David-Matthew Barnes. As rock band the Jetsetters skyrocket from obscurity to superstardom, Justin Holt, a lonely barista, and Diego Delgado, the band's guitarist, fight with everything they have to stay together, despite the chaos and fame. (978-1-60282-745-5)

**Strange Bedfellows** by Rob Byrnes. Partners in life and crime, Grant Lambert and Chase LaMarca are hired to make a politician's compromising photo disappear, but what should be an easy job quickly spins out of control. (978-1-60282-746-2)

**Fontana** by Joshua Martino. Fame, obsession, and vengeance collide in a novel that asks: What if America's greatest hero was gay? (978-1-60282-675-5)

**The Dirty Diner: Gay Erotica on the Menu**, edited by Jerry L. Wheeler. Gay erotica set in restaurants, featuring food, sex, and men—could you really ask for anything more? (978-1-60282-677-9)

**Sweat: Gay Jock Erotica** by Todd Gregory. Sizzling tales of smoking-hot sex with the athletic studs everyone fantasizes about. (978-1-60282-669-4)

**The Marrying Kind** by Ken O'Neill. Just when successful wedding planner Adam More decides to protest inequality by quitting the business and boycotting marriage entirely, his only sibling announces her engagement. (978-1-60282-670-0)

**Calendar Boys** by Logan Zachary. A man a month will keep you excited year-round. (978-1-60282-665-6)